THE FURTHER ADVENTURES OF
NILS

Selma Lagerlöf

Translated by Velma Swanston Howard
Revised by Nancy Johnson

THE TRAVELS OF
BOOK TWO
NILS HOLGERSSON

SKANDISK
MINNEAPOLIS

....

THE WONDERFUL ADVENTURES OF NILS, BOOK TWO:

THE FURTHER ADVENTURES OF NILS

First edition published by Skandisk, Inc. 1992
Skandisk, Inc.
7616 Lyndale Avenue South
Minneapolis, Minnesota 55423

ISBN 0-9615394-4-5

Revised English translation Copyright © 1992 Skandisk, Inc.
Illustrations Copyright © 1947 Pantheon Books Inc.
Original English edition published 1907 by Grosset & Dunlap.
Translated from the original Swedish edition, published 1907 under the title
Nils Holgerssons underbara resa genom Sverige.
Copyright in all countries signatory to the Berne and Universal Conventions.

Text revision: Nancy Johnson
Cover and book design: Koechel Peterson & Associates, Minneapolis, Minnesota.

Manufactured in the United States of America.

Skandisk, Inc., publishes *The Tomten*, a catalog which offers exemplary
children's literature, immigrant books, Scandinavian literature, music and gifts
with a Scandinavian accent. For information write to The Tomten,
7616 Lyndale Avenue South, Minneapolis, Minnesota 55423.

....

Contents

....

Foreword   5

I   **The Story of Karr and Grayskin:** *Karr*   9
Grayskin's Flight   12
Helpless, the Water Snake   16
The Nun Moths   21
The War of the Moths   24
Retribution   29

II   **The Wind Witch:** *In Närke*   37
Market Eve   40

III   **The Breaking up of the Ice**   51

IV   **Thumbietot and the Bears:** *The Ironworks*   57

V   **The Flood:** *The Swans*   71
The New Watchdog   78

VI   **Dunfin:** *The City That Floats on the Water*   83
The Sisters   88

VII   **Stockholm:** *Skansen*   97

VIII   **Gorgo, the Eagle:** *In the Mountain Glen*   115
In Captivity   121

IX   **On Over Gästrikland:** *The Precious Belt*   127
Forest Day   130

X   **A Day in Hälsingland:** *A Large Green Leaf*   135
The Animals' Near Year's Eve   138

XI   **In Medelpad**   151

XII	A Morning in Ångermanland: *The Bread*	159
XIII	Västerbotten and Lapland: *The Five Scouts*	169
	The Moving Landscape	172
	The Dream	174
	The Meeting	179
XIV	Osa, the Goose Girl, and Little Mats	183
XV	With the Laplanders	191
	The Next Morning	193
XVI	Homeward Bound!: *The First Day of Travel*	201
XVII	Legends From Härjedalen	207
XVIII	Värmland and Dalsland	217
	A Little Homestead	218
XIX	The Treasure on the Island:	
	On Their Way *to the Sea*	231
	The Gift of the Wild Geese	233
XX	The Journey to Vemminghög	239
XXI	Home at Last	243
XXII	The Parting With the Wild Geese	253
	Map of Nils' Adventures	258
	Table of Pronunciation	260
	A Final Note	261

Foreword

....

A naughty boy who entered a magical world as Thumbietot (*tummetott*, in Swedish), a tiny imp, and learned the meaning of kindness and courage; a powerful tomten who had his revenge; a gaggle of wise wild geese; and an ornery fox all lived in Sweden a long time ago. They come to life again whenever a child reads *The Wonderful Adventures of Nils*. Commissioned by the Swedish National Teachers' Society as an introductory geography for schoolchildren, this is an adventure story, a folktale, a geography and a history. It's a chain of short narratives, every one of them a masterpiece of the storyteller's art.

Author Selma Lagerlöf's fantasy has enchanted Sweden's children ever since it was first published in 1907 as *Nils Holgerssons underbara resa genom Sverige*. Translated into other languages, the story of Nils Holgersson's travels across Sweden on the back of a white gander is still popular. Germany's children have made it a bast-seller. The 1991 edition of Book One and this 1992 edition of Book Two in the two-volume set, a revision of Velma Swanston Howard's translation from the Swedish, promise to become cherished classics of English-speaking children the world over. As in the first English edition, some of the descriptive geographical detail in the Swedish original has been eliminated. The story itself is complete.

There was something very special about the author, Selma Lagerlöf. She was a novelist, a short story writer, an autobiographer, a poet, a biographer and a dramatist. Herman Hesse, a recipient of the Nobel Prize in literature for 1946, said: "With her first work, *Gösta Berling*, she became famous in Sweden and very soon in the rest of the world. That first work was already perfect, containing all the essentials of the Lagerlöf gift...."

Synthesis of social comment, folklore and historical fact was characteristic of her work, and it is very evident in *The Wonderful Adventures of Nils*. Selma Lagerlöf's saga is as appealing now as when it was first created in the early 1900s. The problems addressed—poverty, sickness, draining of wetlands and deforestation, cruelty to animals and child abuse, for example—are contemporary issues. Before she finished the book, Selma Lagerlöf wrote: "Through my reader, I want the young people to get an accurate picture of their country and to learn to love and understand it; I want them also to learn something about its many resources and the possibilities for development that it offers..." (letter to Josepha Ahnfeldt, November 18, 1904).

The author was born on November 20, 1858, in Mårbacka, Värmland, in southwestern Sweden. Her father was Erik Gustaf, a lieutenant in the Swedish army. Her mother's name, Louisa. Selma was the fourth of five children. The family was "lesser gentry," on friendly speaking terms with the nobility and receiving a certain nod of deference from the peasantry.

In 1863, when Selma was five years old, her grandmother passed away. That was a shock. Selma said: "My one recollection of her is of her sitting there day after day and telling stories from morning till evening.... It was as if the door to a wonderful magic world, in and out of which we had come and gone freely, had been locked...."

From 1881 until 1885 she attended the Stockholm Higher Teacher's College for Women, where she became fascinated with Scandinavian folklore. After her father died in 1885 and the family estate was sold, she supported herself by teaching at the Girls' High School in Landskrona. While there, she wrote her first novel, *Gösta Berling's saga* (*Gösta Berling's Saga*), which was published in 1891.

First the book was criticized for the mingling of fact with fiction. After it was given a favorable review by Danish critic Georg Brandes in 1893, *Gösta Berling's Saga* was reconsidered. Eventually it was applauded as not only Selma Lagerlöf's best novel, but one of the finest in Swedish literature.

Her first short story collection, *Osynliga länka* or *Invisible Links*, published in 1894, made it clear that her writing could be financially successful. She left teaching and became a professional writer. The door that had been locked when her grandmother died was open. Selma was a gifted storyteller, and the Swedish people loved her books. She even gained an international following, particularly for *The Wonderful Adventures of Nils*.

On November 23, 1907, this short paragraph about the

book appeared in the *New York Times* under the title "Exciting Adventures for Boys":

"The Wonderful Adventures of Nils is the last and said to be the best book of Sweden's great fiction writer, Selma Lagerlöf, and the Swedish people say there has been nothing in their literature for children since Hans Christian Andersen to compare with it. It is the result of years of study of animal and bird life by the author, with legends and folklore, which are woven together into the charming story of little Nils, turned into an elf, traveling on the back of a goose with a flock of wild geese, understanding the speech of birds and animals. The book was brought out in Stockholm in December, 1906, and since then has been translated into German and Danish, in which it has been equally well received. It is translated into English by Velma Swanston Howard. There are delightful full-page and marginal pictures by Harold Heartt. (Doubleday, Page & Co.)"

Selma Lagerlöf was famous. In *The Wonderful Adventues of Nils*, she had created a remarkable tale of Sweden. That tale, with all of its insight and childlike delight, will be treasured for as long as there are children to read it.

In 1904 she received the Gold Medal of the Swedish Academy, and in 1914 she was elected the first woman member of that distinctive institution. In 1909 she was awarded the Nobel Prize in literature; she was the first woman ever to receive that honor. She used the money to buy back the entire Mårbacka estate, where she lived for the rest of her life. She died on March 16, 1940, at the age of eighty-one.

BIBLIOGRAPHY
Commire, Anne, ed. *Something About the Author*, Vol. XV, pp. 160-174. Detroit, Michigan: Gale Research Co., 1979.
Kepos, Paula, ed. *Twentieth-Century Literary Criticism*, Vol. XXXVI, pp. 228-249. Detroit, Michigan: Gale Research Inc., 1990.
"Exciting Adventures for Boys," *New York Times*, Vol. XII (November 23, 1907), p. 749.

THE TRAVELS OF
BOOK TWO
NILS HOLGERSSON

Chapter One

The Story of Karr and Grayskin

Karr
....

Twelve years or so before Nils Holgersson began his adventure with the wild geese, a manufacturer at Kolmården wanted to be rid of a dog. The stubborn animal wouldn't stop chasing sheep and birds.

"Take him into the woods and shoot him," he instructed his gamekeeper.

So the gamekeeper put the dog on a leash and led him toward the place where old and sick dogs from the manor were shot and buried. He was not a cruel man, but he fully intended to shoot the dog. Chasing sheep and chickens was bad enough, but they weren't the only animals the dog had hunted. He had poached rabbits and grouse chicks in the forest, too.

Karr was the dog's name. He was a smart little black-and-tan setter—so smart, in fact, that he understood the whole conversation. As the gamekeeper led him through the brush, Karr knew what was supposed to happen; he only pretended not to.

Great stretches of woodland surrounded the factory, and this forest was famous among animals and humans. For years the owners had allowed the trees to grow without thinning or any other interference. Naturally the forest became a wildlife refuge, and the animals called it Liberty Forest. They regarded it as the best retreat in the country.

Karr had caused all kinds of trouble for the small animals and birds who lived there. "Wouldn't they be happy if they knew what the gamekeeper intends to do?" he thought. He wagged his tail and barked cheerfully to hide his feelings. "I don't regret anything I have done."

The moment he uttered the defiant words, Karr thought of

something he did regret. He stretched his neck as if he'd like to howl, and he dragged on the leash.

What an awful secret! It was still early in the summer, and the elk cows had given birth. Just last night, Karr had separated a young calf from its mother and driven it down to the marsh. There he chased it, only five days old, back and forth over the knolls—not to capture it, but to scare it.

Well aware that the bottomless marsh could not bear her massive weight, the mother elk had stood at the edge of the marsh, watching helplessly. When she realized that Karr was chasing her little one farther and farther away, she frantically rushed out to drive the dog off. Then she nudged her calf back toward dry land.

They had almost reached dry ground when the mother slipped, and the mud sucked her down to her death. Instead of helping, Karr ran away. His only worry was the beating he'd get if anyone found out.

The setter thought to himself, "Since the elk cow and calf were alive when I left, maybe they could still be saved."

As soon as the gamekeeper loosened his grip on the leash, Karr yanked it away and ran. He was out of sight before the man could level his gun. Following the sound of his barks and howls, the gamekeeper finally pinpointed Karr out in the marsh.

"What's going on out there?" the gamekeeper wondered. He dropped his gun and crawled out over the marsh. He had not gone far when he saw an elk cow lying dead in the mud. Beside her was a calf, still alive but too weak to move. Karr was licking the calf.

The gamekeeper gently approached the little animal, then dragged it toward more solid ground. Karr jumped around the gamekeeper, yelping with delight. At last they reached safety, and the gamekeeper carried the baby elk home. He laid it in a calf stall in the cow shed. Then he got help to drag the mother elk from the marsh and bury her. Only after all that did he remember why he had gone to the woods in the morning.

The gamekeeper called Karr and again took him into the forest. He seemed pensive.

"I won't be shot after all," Karr tried to convince himself. "The gamekeeper must think I've done a good deed today. "

Suddenly the gamekeeper turned around and walked back toward the manor. Karr had been trotting quietly beside him, but he imagined the worst.

"Oh, no! He must have discovered that I'm responsible for the elk's death. He's taking me back to the manor to tell the master what I've done. Then he will kill me."

The master was standing on the stairs leading to the hall when the gamekeeper walked up to him. "Where did that dog come from?" he asked, surprised. "Is it Karr? Didn't you shoot him this morning?"

The gamekeeper told him about the mother and baby elk. As he talked, Karr crouched behind the man's legs.

"Good dog!" the master exclaimed.

"How can I shoot him now?" asked the gamekeeper.

The master replied, "Well, if you promise to take charge of the dog and answer for his behavior, I will be satisfied."

That was how it happened that Karr moved into the gamekeeper's lodge.

Grayskin's Flight

From the day that Karr went to live with the gamekeeper, he was a different dog. He loved his master. If the man left the house, Karr ran ahead to make sure that the way was clear. If he stayed at home, Karr stood guard in front of the door.

For the first few days after his close call with death, Karr wouldn't leave his master for a moment. He even accompanied him to the cowshed to visit the elk calf. Every time the gamekeeper fed the calf, Karr sat outside the stall.

The gamekeeper called the calf Grayskin, and Karr agreed that it was a good name. The calf had long, gangly legs that hung from his body like loose stilts; a large, wrinkled head that drooped to one side; and loose skin with tucks and folds. The lonely orphan scrambled to its feet every time Karr appeared.

But as time went by, the calf seemed to be dying. At last he was too weak to rise when he saw Karr. The dog's heart softened, and he jumped into the calf's crib to greet him. A spark of happiness kindled in the baby's eyes. After that Karr visited the elk calf every day, spending hours licking his coat, playing and racing with him, until he had taught him a little of everything a forest animal should know.

The calf seemed to be more content, and he was growing. Why, he grew so rapidly that in two weeks the stall could no longer hold him and he had to be moved into a grove.

In two months, the elk's legs were so long that he could step over the fence. Then the lord of the manor gave the gamekeeper permission to install a higher fence and allow Grayskin more space. There the elk lived for several years, growing into a strong and handsome animal. Karr visited him as often as he could, but it was no longer because he felt sorry for him. By now they were close friends.

Grayskin had been on the gamekeeper's place five summers when his owner received a letter from a zoological garden abroad offering to purchase the elk. The owner was glad to get the offer, and he wanted to close the sale immediately. The gamekeeper disagreed with him, but he didn't have the authority to say no.

When Karr told Grayskin that he would be sold, the elk took the news calmly.

"Aren't you going to resist?" Karr asked.

"What good would it do to resist?" Grayskin replied.

The dog looked closely at his friend. The elk was not yet full-grown. He did not have the magnificent antlers, high hump, and heavy dewlap of the mature elk, but he certainly did have the strength to fight for his freedom. Yet, Grayskin could not remember being a free animal so he could not know the value of freedom.

Karr left without another word and did not return to the grove until long past midnight. By that time he knew Grayskin would be awake and eating his breakfast.

The dog said, "You're right, Grayskin. You might as well let the zookeepers come and get you. You'll be a prisoner in a large park, of course, but you won't have any responsibilities. Only, it is sad that you will not have seen the forest. Your ancestors have a saying that the elk are one with the forest. Wouldn't you like to see it...just once before you leave?"

Grayskin glanced up from the clover he was munching on.

"I'd like to see the forest, Karr," he replied, "but how could I get over the fence?"

Karr chuckled. "That would be hard for you."

Grayskin looked at him. Karr, even with his short dog legs, jumped the fence many times a day. Grayskin went over to the fence, and with one spring he was on the other side. The two friends walked slowly into the dark forest.

"Should we turn back?" Karr asked the elk. "Since you have never been in the forest, you might stumble and break your legs."

"Don't worry about me," Grayskin said, and he picked up his pace. He didn't want the terrier to think he was afraid.

Karr led Grayskin far into the forest, where the pines were so thick that the wind could not penetrate them. "Here the wild elk seek shelter from storms and cold. You'll be much better off at the zoo, where you'll stand in a shed like an ox."

Grayskin did not answer him, but stood quietly, drinking in the pine-scented air. "Do you have anything else to show me, or is the whole forest like this?" he asked.

"Come and see." Karr started off again, leading Grayskin to a wide marsh. "There. Look at the quagmire. It's dotted with mounds of earth and grass, like miniature islands. Heavy elk can pick their way across this marsh when they are in danger. Of course, you will never be hounded by hunters, so you have no reason to learn the ways of your ancestors."

With a bound, Grayskin was out into the marsh, feeling the mounds of earth rock back and forth under him. After exploring the marsh without once having stepped into a mudhole, he returned to Karr.

"Have you shown me the whole forest now?" Grayskin asked.

"No, no...not yet," was the dog's reply. Karr took the elk to the skirt of the forest, where oaks, lindens, and aspens grew. "Here the wild elk eat leaves and bark. They consider it the choicest food, but maybe you'll get better food at the zoo."

The Story of Karr and Grayskin

The tame elk was astonished when he found that the enormous canopy of leaves above him was good to eat. After sampling oak leaves and aspen bark, he said, "The leaves are bitter, but they are delicious. They are better than clover."

"I am glad you have had this one opportunity to taste them," the dog said. Then he took Grayskin to a forest lake. The water was as smooth as a mirror and reflected the shores, which were veiled in a light mist. When Grayskin saw the lake, he stood entranced; he had never seen a lake.

"What is this, Karr?"

"It's water—a lake," the dog replied. "The elk swim across it. See what it's like."

Karr jumped in. Grayskin stayed on the shore for awhile, then followed the dog's example. He grew breathless as the cool water stole soothingly around his body. He wanted it over his back, too, so he went farther out. The water held him up, and he swam all around Karr, ducking and snorting. He was perfectly at home in the water. When they were on shore again, the dog asked if they hadn't better go home.

"Morning is a long way off," Grayskin protested. "Let's look around in the forest a little longer."

They went back into the pine wood and entered an open glade illuminated by the moonlight, where grass and flowers shimmered in dew. Large animals were grazing on this forest meadow—an elk bull, several elk cows and their calves. When Grayskin caught sight of them, he stopped short. He hardly glanced at the cows or the young ones, but stared at the old bull. He had wide antlers, a high hump, and a long-haired dewlap hanging from his throat.

"Who is he?" Grayskin asked.

"He is called Antler Crown," Karr said. "He's one of your relatives. One of these days you, too, will have massive antlers and a dewlap. You could have a herd like his to lead."

"I would like to meet him," Grayskin said. Leaving his companion at the edge of the clearing, Grayskin approached the bull elk and greeted him. Almost immediately he returned to Karr.

"You weren't well received, were you."

The elk shook his head. "No. I told him that this was the first time to my memory that I had seen any of my kind. When I asked him if I might accompany him, he drove me back, threatening me with his antlers."

"You backed off? Any other young bull would have felt disgraced if he had retreated without resistance. I guess that's not your concern. You are going to a foreign country."

Grayskin turned. The old elk came toward him, and the two began to spar. Their antlers met and clashed, and Grayskin was driven across the meadow. When he reached the edge of the forest, he planted his hooves on the ground, pushed hard with his antlers, and stopped Antler Crown's advance.

Grayskin fought silently, while Antler Crown puffed and snorted. The old elk, in his turn, was now forced back over the meadow. Part of the old elk's antlers snapped. He tore loose, and crashed into the forest.

Karr was waiting for the victor. "Now that you have seen the forest, Grayskin, are you ready to return to the gamekeeper's pen?"

He was saddened to hear his friend reply, "Yes, it's about time."

Both were silent on the way home. Karr sighed several times. Grayskin walked ahead unhesitatingly until they reached the enclosure. He looked at the narrow pen where he had lived for five years, saw the beaten ground, the stale fodder, the water trough, and the dark shed.

Raising his broad, curved muzzle, he trumpeted, "The elk are one with the forest!" and loped into the woods.

Helpless, the Water Snake

Every year, in the month of August, in a pine thicket in the heart of Liberty Forest, some grayish-white nun moths appeared. After fluttering about the forest a couple of nights, they laid a few thousand eggs on tree branches, and not long afterward, the moths dropped lifeless to the ground.

When spring came, prickly caterpillars crawled out of the eggs and began to eat the pine needles. They had good appetites, but they didn't do the leaves much damage because they were chased by birds. Only a few hundred caterpillars ever escaped.

Those that lived to be full-grown crawled up on the branches, spun white webs around themselves, and sat motionless for two weeks. During this time, as a rule, more than half of them were abducted. If a hundred nun moths emerged in August, winged and perfect, it was reckoned a good year for them.

For many years the nun moths led this sort of uncertain and obscure existence in Liberty Forest. They would have remained quite harmless, but as it happened, Grayskin's introduction to the forest had something to do with a strange calamity.

One day, when Grayskin was roaming the forest, he happened to squeeze through a thicket behind a clearing. Before he could back out, he was standing in mud. In front of him was a slimy, smelly pool of stagnant water. If he hadn't seen some bright-green calla leaves growing near the pool, Grayskin would have left immediately.

Arching his neck to reach the calla stalks, he disturbed a black snake sleeping underneath them. The snake raised her head and hissed. Remembering Karr's warning about poisonous adders, Grayskin was terrified. He reared and crushed the snake's head with one blow of a hoof. Then he turned and fled.

Another snake, as long and as black, slithered up from the pool to the dead one.

"Are you dead, my dear Harmless?" hissed the snake. "We have lived together so many years…been so happy…gotten along so well in the swamp. We have lived to be older than all the other water snakes in the forest." The snake writhed in sorrow. Even the frogs, who lived in constant fear of Helpless, felt sorry for him.

"What a wicked creature!" Helpless raged. "He murdered a defenseless water snake. As sure as my name is Helpless and I am the oldest water snake in the forest, I will be avenged. I will not rest until that bull elk lies dead like my mate."

Old Helpless coiled up and pondered what action to take.

He thought for days without finding a solution. Then one night as he lay dreaming of vengeance, he noticed nun moths flitting among the trees. He watched them a long while, hissing thoughtfully. Finally he fell asleep, pleased with an idea that had occurred to him.

The next morning the water snake slithered over to see Crawlie, the adder who lived in a stony, hilly part of Liberty Forest. Helpless told Crawlie all about the death of Harmless and begged him to bite the bull elk with his venomous fangs.

"If I attacked an elk," said the adder, "he would kill me. Old Harmless is gone. We can't bring her back to life, so why should I endanger myself on her account?"

The water snake raised his head a foot from the ground and hissed, "Vish vash! Vish vash! You miserable coward."

"Crawl away, old Helpless," the adder warned. "You've insulted me once, and you'll never have another chance. Poison is already dripping from my fangs. One bite...but I'd rather not kill you."

Helpless did not move, and for a long time the snakes hissed abusive epithets at each other. When Crawlie was so angry that he could no longer hiss, but only dart his tongue, old Helpless changed the subject.

Lowering his voice to a whisper, the water snake said, "There is another way to avenge my dear Harmless, but I suppose you are too angry to listen."

"As long as you don't ask me to do anything foolish, I will help you," the adder relented.

"There are nun moths in the pine trees down by the swamp."

"What about them?" Crawlie hissed.

"They are the smallest insect family in the forest. They are

the most harmless, too, because the caterpillars only gnaw on pine needles."

"So?" questioned Crawlie.

"I am afraid they will be exterminated," the water snake sighed. "So many pick off the caterpillars in the spring."

Now Crawlie understood Helpless' train of thought, and there was a wicked gleam in his eye. "Would you like me to ask the owls to leave those poor pine tree worms in peace?"

"Yes, I would. You have authority in the forest. You make the request."

"Don't you think it would be a nice idea to drop a good word for the pine needle pickers among the thrushes as well?" Crawlie suggested.

Helpless hissed in satisfaction. "I am glad I came to you, Crawlie."

The Nun Moths

One morning in early summer, some years later, Karr lay asleep on the porch. Night lights made the sky as bright as day although the sun was not yet up.

"Karr!"

Karr opened his eyes and looked around.

"Karr!"

"Is that you, Grayskin?" the dog asked. He was used to the elk's nightly visits. He got up and hurried in the direction of the sound. Karr heard the elk's footfalls in the distance, as he plunged into the pine wood, straight through the brush. Karr could not catch up with him and even had difficulty following the trail.

"Karr, Karr!"

The voice was certainly Grayskin's, but it sounded strange.

"I'm coming! I'm coming, Grayskin. Where are you?"

"Karr! Don't you see how the needles fall and fall?"

Then the dog noticed that pine needles were dropping from the trees, like a steady fall of rain. "Yes, I see the needles falling," he cried, and ran far into the forest in search of the elk.

"Karr, Karr!" Grayskin roared, his nostrils flaring. "Do you smell that odd odor in the forest?"

Karr stopped and sniffed. "Yes, I catch the scent," he said.

"Karr, Karr… Do you hear crunching on the pines?" Now Grayskin's tone could have melted a stone.

Karr paused to listen. He heard a faint but distinct "tap, tap" on the trees. It sounded like the ticking of a watch.

"Yes, I hear the sound," Karr answered. Standing still beneath the drooping branches of a great pine, the dog looked carefully at the pine needles. The needles moved. He looked more closely. A mass of grayish-white caterpillars were creeping along the branches, gnawing off needles. Every branch was covered with them. The crunch, crunch in the trees came from their busy little jaws chewing, chewing, chewing. Gnawed-off pine needles fell to the ground in a continuous shower, and a horrid odor rose from them, offending the dog's sensitive nose.

"A plague of caterpillars! Why is this happening? Our beautiful trees will be stripped bare." Karr went from tree to tree, trying to find a tree that was untouched, but the caterpillars had swarmed over every tree he could see. "The gamekeeper won't be pleased with this," he thought.

Karr ran deeper into the thickets, anxious to learn how far the plague had spread. Wherever he went, he heard the same ticking, smelled the same odor, saw the same rain of needles. The caterpillars were everywhere.

"But no, not here." Karr had come to a tract where there was no odor and no ticking sound. Stripped of every needle, the trees were already dying. A network of ragged threads hung on them—the roads and bridges of tiny caterpillars.

And there, among the dying pines, stood Grayskin. He was not alone. With him were four old elk—the most respected elk in the forest. Karr knew them. They were Crooked Back, who was a small elk, but had a larger hump than the others; Antler Crown, the most dignified of the elk; Rough Mane, with the thick coat; and an old, long-legged one, who until the autumn before, when he had gotten a bullet in his thigh, had been hot-tempered. His name was Big-and-Strong.

"What caused the plague?" Karr asked. The elk stood with lowered heads and protruding upper lips. They looked puzzled and worried.

"No one knows," Grayskin answered. "The nun moths never used to damage the trees, but within the past few years they have multiplied at an astonishing rate. They could destroy the whole forest."

"Yes, but I see that the wisest animals in the forest have come together to discuss what is happening. Have you decided what to do?"

Crooked Back solemnly raised his head, pricked up his long ears, and said, "Karr, we have summoned you here to learn if the humans are aware of this desolation."

"No," Karr said. "No human being would come this far into the forest until hunting season opens. They don't know anything about this."

Then Antler Crown said, "We can't stop the insect plague without help from the humans."

"This is the end of peace in the forest." Rough Mane moaned.

"We can't allow Liberty Forest to perish," Big-and-Strong protested. "The humans have to be consulted. There's no alternative."

"Do you want me to let the people know the conditions here?" Karr suggested. The old elk nodded their heads.

In a moment, the little black-and-tan terrier was dashing toward home on his important errand. Suddenly a big, black water snake slithered onto the forest path.

"Well met in the forest," the snake hissed.

"Well met again," snarled Karr, without stopping.

"Wait!"

"What does that old snake want?" Karr wondered. "Maybe he's worried about the forest, too." He slowed down and waited for the snake.

"What's this about talking to humans?" old Helpless demanded. "There'll be trouble in the forest the day they interfere."

"I am afraid there will," the dog agreed, "but the oldest forest dwellers know what they are doing."

"I have a better plan," hissed Helpless, "that is, if I get the reward I wish."

"Isn't your name Helpless? Don't you have that name for a good reason?" the dog said contemptuously.

"I am an old inhabitant of the forest, too," Helpless reminded Karr, "and I know how to get rid of the insect plague without turning to humans for help."

"If you do, you can choose your reward." the dog said.

The snake did not reply until he had crawled under a tree stump, where he was protected. Then he said, "Tell Grayskin that if he leaves Liberty Forest forever and goes far north, where no oak tree grows, I will send sickness and death to all the creeping things that gnaw the pines and spruces."

"What?" asked Karr, bristling. "What harm has Grayskin ever done you?"

"He murdered the one I loved most," the snake declared, "and I want him to be punished."

Karr would have made an end to him, but the reptile was safely hidden under the tree stump.

"Stay there, then. The caterpillars will be driven out without your assistance."

The War of the Moths

The next spring, as Karr was running through the woods one morning, he saw an old fox standing outside his lair.

"Karr," the fox called. "Are the humans doing anything?"

"They're doing what they can."

"They have killed all my relatives since they entered the forest," the fox whined, "but I will forgive them if they save the forest."

That year Karr never went into the woods without someone asking if the humans could conquer the moths and save the forest. The dog could only say that the people weren't sure.

Every day more than a hundred men went into Liberty Forest, the great woodland of Kolmården. They cleared the underbrush. They felled dead trees, lopped off branches from the live ones so that the caterpillars could not easily crawl from tree to tree. They dug wide trenches around the ravaged parts and put up lime-washed fences to keep the caterpillars out of new territory. They painted rings of lime around tree trunks to prevent the caterpillars from leaving trees they had already stripped. The idea was to force the caterpillars to remain where they were until they starved to death.

People worked far into the spring, hoping that when the caterpillars came out of their eggs, most of them would die of starvation. They were wrong. By early summer, there were more caterpillars than ever.

They were everywhere. They crawled on the country roads, on fences, on the walls of cabins. They wandered outside of Liberty Forest to other parts of Kolmården.

"They won't stop till all our forests are destroyed," the people said in alarm. Karr was so sick of the creeping, gnawing things that he could hardly bear to go near the forest. At the same time, he was anxious to know how Grayskin was doing.

Karr took the shortest path to the elk's territory. He hurried along, his nose close to the earth. When he came to the tree stump where he had met Helpless the year before, the snake was still there.

"Have you told Grayskin what I said to you last year?" Helpless hissed. Karr only growled and tried to get at him.

"If you have not told him, tell him now. The humans cannot help. Only I can stop the plague."

"You can't do anything," retorted the dog, and ran on.

Karr found Grayskin, but the elk was so depressed that he scarcely greeted his friend. "I don't know what I would not give to bring all this misery to an end," Grayskin moaned.

"Old Helpless the water snake says you can save the forest," Karr said.

"What?" the bull elk questioned, his eyes big with wonder.

"If you leave Liberty Forest forever, going far north beyond the region of oak trees, Helpless says he will destroy the nun moths."

"Why? What do the moths have to do with me?" Grayskin asked.

"Helpless said you killed the one he loved most."

"What? Oh, bosh! Anyway, how could an old water snake save our forest?"

"He is bluffing," said Karr. "Water snakes always pretend they know more than any other animal."

When Karr was ready to go home, Grayskin agreed to accompany him part of the way. As they walked through the forest, they heard a thrush perched on top of a pine top cry: "Here comes Grayskin, who destroyed our forest. Here comes Grayskin, who destroyed our forest." Karr thought he must have been mistaken. What had he heard?

The next moment a hare darted across their path. When he saw the dog and his companion, he stopped, flapped his ears, and screamed: "Here comes Grayskin, who destroyed the forest." Then he ran off as fast as he could.

"What did he mean by that?" asked Karr.

"I'm not sure," said Grayskin. "I think the small forest animals are angry because I proposed that we ask humans to help us. When the underbrush was cut down, all the lairs and hiding places were destroyed."

"Grayskin destroyed the forest! Grayskin destroyed the forest!" The cries came from all directions. Grayskin pretended not to hear it, and Karr felt sorry for him.

"Grayskin, what did Helpless mean when he said you killed the one he loved most?"

"How can I tell?" said Grayskin. "I never kill anything."

Karr nodded, "I know," and they went on their way. A few minutes later, they met the four old elk—Crooked Back, Antler Crown, Rough Mane, and Big-and-Strong—who were coming along slowly, one after the other.

"Well met in the forest," called Grayskin.

"Well met in turn," answered the elk.

One said, "We were looking for you, Grayskin, to talk with you about the forest."

"The fact is," began Crooked Back, "we have been informed that a crime has been committed and that the whole forest is being destroyed because the criminal has not been punished."

"What kind of crime?"

"Someone killed a harmless creature that he couldn't eat. Such an act is accounted a crime in Liberty Forest."

"Who would have done that?" asked Grayskin.

"They say that an elk did it, and we were going to ask you if you knew who it was."

"No," said Grayskin, "I've never heard of an elk killing a harmless creature."

The friends parted without another word. Inconsolable, Grayskin went on with Karr. They happened to pass Crawlie the adder, who lay on his rock shelf.

"There goes Grayskin, who destroyed the whole forest," hissed Crawlie like all the rest.

Grayskin's patience was gone. He turned to the adder and raised a hoof.

"Do you intend to crush me like you crushed poor Harmless, the water snake?"

"Did I kill a water snake?" Grayskin asked, astonished.

"The first day you were in the forest you killed the wife of old Helpless."

Grayskin looked back at Karr, exclaiming, "I committed the crime! So it's because of me that the forest is being destroyed."

"No!" Karr objected. "I don't believe it."

"Tell Helpless the water snake that Grayskin will go into exile tonight."

"No, I won't! The Far North is too dangerous for elk."

"Karr, you taught me that the elk are one with the forest." With that, Grayskin left his friend.

The dog went home alone, but the next morning he returned to the forest to look for Grayskin. The elk was not to be found, but the gamekeeper was there. Karr saw him pointing up at a tree.

"What are you looking at?" asked a man who stood beside him.

"The caterpillars seem to be sick," observed the gamekeeper with surprise.

"I think you're right. They do look sick."

"Then the water snake kept his word," Karr murmured to himself. "As soon as Helpless has cleaned out the caterpillars, I know someone who is going to bite his head off."

It was true that the caterpillars were sick, but the plague did not come to an end overnight. The larvae turned into pupae, and from them came millions of moths. They flew around in the trees like a snowstorm, and they laid more eggs. Even greater deforestation was forecast for the coming year.

The destruction came not only to the forest, but to the caterpillars as well. Sickness spread from forest to forest. Caterpillars stopped eating, crawled up to the branches of the trees, and died there.

Karr thought of the day when the forest would be saved. Then he could kill Helpless and call his old friend home from exile in the Far North. Two more summers went by before that time came.

Grayskin sent messages to Karr to tell him that he was alive and getting along fine, but birds told Karr confidentially that Grayskin had been pursued by poachers on several occasions. Only with the greatest difficulty had he escaped. The elk was past his prime.

The two summers made a difference in the brave little black-and-tan terrier, too. He could no longer hunt, he could not run, he could not track his enemy, and he could not see at all. Karr didn't have the strength to kill a water snake. How could he help Grayskin now?

....

Retribution

....

One afternoon, Akka from Kebnekaise and her flock landed on the shore of a forest lake. Spring was slow in coming, as it always is in the mountain districts. Except for a narrow strip along the edge, the lake was covered with ice.

The geese plunged into the water to bathe and hunt for food. Nils Holgersson, who had lost a wooden shoe early that morning, walked along the shore to look for something to bind around his foot.

He glanced nervously around him. "Oh, if only I were on the plains," he thought. "Then I would be able to see if anyone were coming. I'd be better off if this were a grove of little birches, because then the ground would be almost bare; how people can like these wild, pathless forests is hard for me to understand. If I owned this land, I would chop down every tree.

"Oh, there's a piece of birch bark that I can use." Just as he was fastening it onto his foot, he heard a rustle behind him. He turned quickly. A snake darted from the bush straight toward him. The snake was long and thick, but the boy saw that it had a white spot on each cheek.

"You're just a water snake. You can't hurt me," the boy taunted. The snake struck him on the chest, knocking him down. Nils was on his feet in a second, running, but the snake followed close at his heels. Nils saw a huge boulder and climbed to the top of it.

The snake slithered up after him. Close to Nils, on a narrow ledge at the top of the boulder, was a round rock as large as a man's head. Nils scurried behind the rock and gave it a push. The rock rolled down on the snake, drawing it along down to the ground, where it landed on its head.

"Whew! The snake almost had me," Nils thought. "Thank goodness for that rock." He watched the snake squirm a little, and then it lay still.

"I don't think I've been in more danger on the whole trip," he said.

"Squawk!"

"What?" Nils looked up, startled. "Why, it's a raven."

The bird was circling overhead. After a couple of minutes, it lighted on the ground right beside the water snake. The bird was like a crow in size and shape, but it was dressed in a pretty coat of shiny black feathers.

Nils cautiously retreated into a crevice of the boulder. His abduction by the crows was still fresh in his memory, and he did not intend to tempt the raven by standing in full view.

The bird strode back and forth beside the snake's body, then turned it over with his beak. Finally he spread his wings and shrieked, "Helpless the water snake is dead! He's dead!" Once more he walked the length of the snake. Then he stood in a deep study, scratching his neck with his foot.

"There cannot be two big snakes like this in the forest," he decided. "No, this must be old Helpless." The raven was about to dine on the snake, but suddenly checked himself.

"Bataki, you numskull," he said, "you must not eat the snake until you have told Karr what's happened to his enemy. He would never believe it if he did not see the snake him-self."

Nils had tried to keep quiet, but the bird looked so funny, strut-ting so solemnly around the dead water snake, that he had to laugh.

Bataki heard him and with a flap of his wings, was up on the boulder beside the boy.

"Are you the one called Bataki, the raven?" Nils asked.

The bird nodded.

"Aren't you a friend of Akka from Kebnekaise?"

The bird nodded again. He took a good look at the boy, then asked, "Are you Thumbietot, the little chap who flies with the wild geese?"

"Oh, you know of me," the boy said proudly.

"Well, then, Thumbietot, did you see how the old water snake met his death?"

"I rolled a rock down on him, and it killed him," the boy responded. He told Bataki how the snake had chased him and how he had feared for his life.

"You may be tiny, but you are clever," the raven remarked. "I have a friend who will be glad to know that this snake has been killed. How can I thank you for this service?"

Nils responded, "Tell me why you are glad the water snake is dead."

"Oh, it is a long story," the raven said. "You would not have the patience to listen to it."

Nils insisted that he had, so the raven told him the whole story about Karr and Grayskin and Helpless the water snake. When he was done, the boy sat quietly for a moment, looking straight ahead. Then he said, "I wonder if there is anything left of Liberty Forest."

"Most of it has been destroyed, " Bataki said. "The trees look black and bare as if they had gone through a fire. They will have to be cleared away. Many years will pass before the forest is lush and healthy again."

"That snake deserved his death," Nils said. "Do you really think he saved the forest?"

"I don't know. Helpless may have known that the caterpillars would eventually sicken and die."

"That may be. All the same, he was a wily snake." Nils stopped talking because he saw the raven was no longer listening to him.

"Shh. There. Do you hear him? Karr is in the forest. Won't he be relieved when he sees that Helpless is dead?"

The boy turned his head in the direction of the barking. "I think the dog is talking with the wild geese," he said.

"Oh, you may be sure he has crawled down to the strand to get the latest news about Grayskin," Bataki said.

Both the boy and the raven jumped to the ground and hastened down to the shore. All the geese had come out of the water and stood talking with an old dog, who was so weak and crippled that it seemed as though he could not live much longer.

"Thumbietot," said the raven, "let Karr hear what the geese have to say. Afterward we will tell him about the water snake."

Akka, the lead goose, was relating an experience the flock had last spring. "Yksi, Kaksi and I started out one morning," she said, "and we flew over the great boundary forests between Dalecarlia and Hälsingland. Under us were thick pine forests. The snow was still deep among the trees, and the creeks were mostly frozen.

"All seemed quiet until we noticed three poachers on skis. They had dogs on leashes, and they carried knives in their belts. There was a hard crust on the snow, so they did not need to use the forest paths. Apparently they had a definite destination in mind because they skied straight ahead without a pause.

"We wanted to know what the poachers were after, so we circled up and down, looking through the trees. Then, in a dense thicket, we saw three elk—a bull and two cows. They seemed to be resting.

"When we landed near them, the elk bull rose and came toward us. He was the most superb animal we had ever seen. When he realized that it was only some wild geese who had awakened him, he lay down again.

"'No, Granddaddy! Don't go back to sleep,' I cried. 'Get away as fast as you can. Poachers are headed here.'

"'Thank you for your warning, goose mother,' he replied, 'but we are under the protection of the law this time of year. The poachers must be out for fox.'

"'Believe me, old granddaddy, they are coming to attack

you. They do not have guns—only spears and knives. They would not dare fire a shot that someone might hear.'

"The elk bull lay there calmly, but the elk cows were uneasy. 'It may be as the geese say,' they said, 'and began to get up.'

"'Lie down!' the old bull commanded. 'No poachers are coming here.'

"There was nothing more that we could do. We flew up and circled over the place to see what would happen. We had barely risen above the trees when we saw the elk bull leave the thicket. He sniffed the air, then walked toward the poachers. He was standing in the middle of a big, barren marsh, nothing hiding him from view.

"When the poachers emerged from the woods, he fled with the dogs and men right behind him.

"The elk threw back his head and loped as fast as he could. He kicked up snow until it flew like a blizzard around him. Then the elk stopped as if to wait for them to catch up. When they were within sight, he went on ahead. By then we realized that he was luring the poachers away from his cows. He was very brave, to put himself in danger so that his dear ones would remain safe. None of us wanted to leave until we saw how this ended.

"The chase continued for two hours or more. Ordinarily poachers would never catch an elk—he would be too fast and tireless for them—but we could see that the old elk was tiring. Every time he lifted his hooves, we saw blood in his tracks. The elk was heavy, and with every step he sank to the bottom of the hard snow. The icy crust scraped the fur from his legs and tore out pieces of flesh, so he was tortured every time he put a hoof down.

"The poachers and dogs, who were light enough for the snow to hold their weight, pursued him relentlessly. At last the elk bull turned to fight them. He happened to glance up. When he saw us circling above, he called: 'Stay here, wild geese, until this duel is over. The next time you fly over Kolmården, look up the terrier named Karr and ask him if he does not think that his friend Grayskin has met with an honorable end.'"

The Story of Karr and Grayskin

When Akka reached this part of her account, old Karr rose and drew closer to her. "Grayskin led a good life," Karr said. "He understood me. He knew that I would be glad to hear that he acted bravely. Now tell me how—" He raised his tail and held his head back as if to give himself a bold and proud bearing. Then he collapsed.

"Karr! Karr! Come, old friend," called a man's voice from the forest.

The dog rose obediently. "My master is calling me," he said, "and I must not stay longer. I saw him load his gun. Now we two will go into the forest for the last time.

"Thank you, Akka of Kebnekaise. I know my friend Grayskin has died honorably, and now I too can die in peace."

Chapter Two

The Wind Witch

In Närke

L ong ago there was something to be found in Närke that could not be found anywhere else. It was the witch named Ysätter-Kaisa. She had been given the name Kaisa because she stirred up wind and storms. The other name, Ysätter, had been given to her because she was supposed to have come from Ysätter swamp in Asker parish. Her real home must have been at Asker, but she could be seen anywhere in Närke.

Ysätter-Kaisa was no dark, sad witch. She was just the opposite—cheerful and fun-loving. What she liked most of all was a gale. As soon as there was enough wind to suit her, she would fly to the Närke plain to dance. On days when a whirlwind swept the plain, oh, those were the days when Ysätter-Kaisa had fun! She would stand in the wind and spin around, her long hair flying among the clouds and the long trail of her robe sweeping the ground like a dust cloud, with the whole plain spread out under her like a ballroom floor.

Some mornings Ysätter-Kaisa would sit in some tall pine at the top of a precipice and look across the plain. If it happened to be winter and she saw teams of horses on the roads, she would blow up a blizzard, piling drifts so high that people could barely get home by evening. If it chanced to be summer and good harvest weather, Ysätter-Kaisa would sit quietly until the first hayracks had been loaded. Then down she would come with a couple of heavy showers, which put an end to the work for the day.

She was a troublemaker. The charcoal burners up in the Kil mountains hardly dared to take a catnap; as soon as she saw an unwatched kiln, she stole up and blew on it until it roared into a great flame. If metal drivers from Laxå and Svartå were out late in the evening, Ysätter-Kaisa would veil the roads and the country round about in such dark clouds that both men and horses lost their way and drove the heavy wagons into swamps.

If on a summer day the dean's wife at Glanshammar spread the tea table in the garden and along came a gust of wind that lifted the cloth from the table and turned over cups and saucers, she knew who had raised the mischief. If the mayor of Örebro's hat blew off so he had to run across the whole square after it, if the wash on the line blew away and was covered with dirt, or if smoke poured into a cabin and seemed unable to find its way out through the chimney, it was easy enough to guess who was having fun at others' expense.

Although Ysätter-Kaisa the wind witch was fond of all sorts of tantalizing games, she was not really mean. One could see that she was hardest on people who were quarrelsome, stingy, or wicked. She would be kind to honest folk and poor little children. Old people say of her that once when Asker Church was set on fire, Ysätter-Kaisa swept through the air, lit amid fire and smoke on the church roof, and blew out the flames.

All the same, the people of Närke were often irritated by Ysätter-Kaisa. That didn't stop her from playing tricks on them. As she sat on the edge of a cloud and looked down at Närke, which rested so peacefully and comfortably beneath her, she must have thought, "The inhabitants would grow sleepy and dull if it were not for me to rouse them and keep them in good spirits."

Chattering like a magpie, she would rush off, dancing and spinning from one end of the plain to the other. When a Närke

man saw her come dragging her dust trail over the plain, he couldn't help smiling. Provoking though she certainly was, she had a happy spirit. It was just as refreshing for the peasants to meet Ysätter-Kaisa as it was for the plain to be lashed by the windstorm.

Oh, it is said that Ysätter-Kaisa is dead and gone, like all other witches. I cannot believe it. It is as though someone were to say that from now on the air will always be still on the plain and the wind will never again dance across it with blustering breezes and drenching showers.

No, whoever thinks that Ysätter-Kaisa is dead may as well hear what happened in Närke the year that Nils Holgersson traveled through. See what the doubter thinks after he has heard about that.

Market Eve

Wednesday, April twenty-seventh.

It was the day before the big Cattle Fair at Örebro. Rain poured in torrents, and people thought, "This is exactly like it was in Ysätter-Kaisa's time. At fairs she used to be more mischievous than usual. It was quite like her to arrange a downpour like this on the night before a market fair."

As the day wore on, the rain increased. Toward evening there were regular cloudbursts. The roads were like bottomless swamps. Farmers who had started from home early in the morning, so they'd arrive with their cattle and oxen at a reasonable hour, had a hard time. The animals were so tired they could hardly move. Many of them collapsed on the road. People whose homes were along the road had to shelter the market-bound travelers as well as they could. Farmhouses, barns and sheds were soon crowded.

Those who still struggled along toward the inn to stay for the night were disappointed when they arrived. All of the cribs in the barn and all of the stalls in the stable were occupied. The farmers had no choice but to leave their horses and cattle out in the rain. Their masters could barely manage to get under cover themselves.

The crush and mud and slush in the barnyard were frightful. Some of the animals were standing in puddles; they couldn't even lie down. There were thoughtful masters, of course, who procured straw for their animals and spread blankets over them; others, who sat in the inn, drinking and gambling, never gave a moment's thought to the dumb creatures they should have protected.

That evening, the boy and the wild geese had reached a wooded island in Hjälmar Lake. The island was separated from the mainland by a narrow, shallow stream. At low tide, one could pass over it without getting the least bit wet.

Nils could not sleep with the water dripping on him, so he got up and walked around the island. He came upon a horse wandering in the trees. Never in all his life had he seen such a wreck of a horse. The animal was broken-winded and stiff-kneed and so thin that every rib could be seen under the hide. He had neither harness nor saddle, but only a bridle, from which dangled a half-knotted rope-end. Obviously he had had no difficulty in breaking loose from a tether.

The horse walked straight toward the place where the wild geese were sleeping. Nils was afraid he might step on them.

"Watch where you're going!" he shouted.

"There you are!" exclaimed the horse. "I've walked miles to meet you."

"To meet me?" asked the boy, astonished.

"I have ears even if I am old. I have heard many people talk about you." As he spoke, the horse bent his head for a better look at the little tomten. The boy noticed that he had a small head, beautiful eyes, and a soft, sensitive nose.

"He must have been a good horse to begin with, although he has come to grief in his old age," Nils thought.

"I wish you would help me with something," the horse pleaded.

Nils did not want to, so he excused himself on account of the bad weather.

"You will be no worse off on my back than you are standing here," said the horse. "Maybe you don't dare to go with an old horse like me."

"Don't dare! Certainly I dare," said the boy.

"Then wake the geese so that we can arrange a place for them to pick you up tomorrow," replied the horse.

The boy was soon on the horse's back, and he found that the animal trotted well. It was a long ride in the rain and darkness before they stopped near a large inn. The wagon wheel tracks were so deep that Nils was afraid he might drown if he fell into them. Some forty horses and cattle huddled alongside a fence that enclosed the yard. Wagons were piled with packing cases holding sheep, calves, hogs and chickens.

The horse walked over to the fence and halted. Nils saw

how miserable and wet the animals were. He asked, "Why are you standing out here in the rain?"

"We were on our way to a fair at Örebro, but we had to stop here because of the rain. This is an inn, but there is no room for us in the barns."

Nils didn't answer, but sat quietly looking around. Not many of the animals were asleep, and on all sides he heard complaints. The weather was worse than it was earlier in the day. The freezing rain was turning to snow.

"Thumbietot, do you see that fine farmyard over there?" remarked the horse.

"Yes, I see it," answered the boy, "and I can't understand why the people there haven't offered you shelter."

"The people who live on that farm are so stingy and selfish that it would be useless for anyone to ask them for help."

"Then you will have to stay where you are," Nils said. "There is nothing I can do to help."

"I was born and raised on that farm," said the horse. "I know that there is a large barn and a big cowshed, with many empty stalls and mangers. Could you get us in there?"

"I don't think so," Nils said, but he hesitated. He felt so sorry for the poor animals that he decided to try. He ran to the barnyard and found that all the outhouses were locked and the keys gone. He stood there, puzzled and helpless, when aid came to him from an unexpected source. Wind came sweeping along with terrific force and flung open a shed door right in front of him.

Nils ran back to his companion. "It's impossible to get into the barn or the cowhouse," he said, "but a big, empty hayshed is open. I can lead you into that."

"Thank you," said the horse. "It will feel good to sleep on familiar ground. It is the only happiness I can expect in this life."

Meanwhile, at the farm opposite the inn, the family sat up much later than usual that evening. The master of the place was a man of thirty-five, tall and dignified, with a handsome but somber face. He had been out in the rain and gotten wet like everyone else, and at supper he asked his old mother to light a fire on the hearth so he could dry his clothes. The mother kindled a few embers. Then the master hung his coat on the back of a chair and placed it by the fire. With one foot on top of the andiron and a hand resting on his knee, he stood gazing into the embers. There he stood for two whole hours, making no move other than to throw a log on the fire now and then.

The mistress removed the supper things and turned down his bed for the night before she went to her own room and sat down to rest. At intervals she went to the door and looked wonderingly at her son.

"It is nothing to worry about, Mother. I am only thinking," he said. His thoughts were on something that had happened only a short while before. When he passed the inn, a horse dealer had asked him if he would like to purchase a horse. The dealer showed him a weatherbeaten old nag.

"Do you take me for a fool?" he had asked.

"No, no, of course not," said the horse dealer. "I only thought that since the horse once belonged to you, you might care enough to give him a comfortable home in his old age."

He had looked at the horse and recognized it as one he had raised and trained, but it did not occur to him to purchase the animal because of that. Of course not!

Even so, the sight of the horse had awakened memories that bothered him. The horse had been a fine animal. His father had let him tend it from the start. He had loved it more than anything else. His father had complained that he fed it too well, and often he had been obliged to steal out and smuggle oats to it.

Once when he tried to talk with his father about letting him buy a broadcloth suit, or having the cart painted, his father stood as if petrified. He thought the old man would have a stroke. He tried to make his father understand that when he had a fine horse to drive, he would look presentable himself. His father made no reply, but two days later he took the horse to Örebro and sold it.

It was cruel, but it was plain that his father had worried that the horse might cause him to become extravagant. And now, so many years later, he had to admit that his father was right. A horse like that would have been a temptation. At first he had grieved. Many times he went down to Örebro just to stand on a street corner and wait for the horse to pass by, or to steal into the stable and give him a lump of sugar. He thought, "If I ever get the farm, the first thing I do will be to buy back my horse."

Now his father was gone and he had been master for two years, yet he had not attempted to buy the horse. He hadn't even thought of him until today. He knew, of course, that his father was stingy. He also knew that it was better to live on a debt-free place and be called stingy than to carry heavy mortgages like other farm owners.

Suddenly he heard a high-pitched, whining sound, as though someone were mocking him: "It's better to keep a firm hold on one's purse and be called stingy than to be in debt like other farm owners." Angrily, he turned to see who was teasing him, but decided that he had mistaken the howling wind for a human voice.

The hall clock struck eleven. "I should be in bed," the master thought, "but I'd better check the farmyard, to make sure all the doors are closed and all the lights are out. He pulled on his coat and went out into the storm.

He found everything as it should be except that the door to the empty hayshed had been blown open by the wind. He stepped inside for the key, locked the shed door and put the key into his coat pocket. Then he went back to the house, removed his coat, and hung it by the fire.

Something else bothered him. Instead of going to bed, he paced the floor. The storm outside with its biting wind and snow-blended rain was terrible, and his old horse was standing in the storm without even a blanket for protection. He should at least have given his old friend a roof over his head since he had traveled so far.

At the inn, while untying the animals, the boy heard an old wall clock strike eleven times. When all were ready, they marched to the stingy farmer's place across from the inn, with the boy as their guide. But while Nils had been getting the animals together, the farmer had locked the hayshed. When the animals came looking for shelter, the door was closed. Nils was dismayed. Now he had to go into the house and find the key.

"Keep everyone quiet while I go in and get the key," he told the old horse, and off he ran. In front of the house, he noticed two little girls stopping in front of the inn. He ran toward them.

"Come now, Britta Maja," said one. "Do not cry anymore. We are at the inn. Surely the people here will let us in."

Nils shouted, "Do not try to get in there. It is impossible. Try the farmhouse over there, "and he pointed at the stingy farmer's place. There are no guests there."

The little girls heard the words distinctly although they could not see the one who spoke them. They were not very surprised by that since the night was as black as pitch. The older of the two girls promptly answered, "We do not want to go there. The people there are stingy and cruel. It's their fault that we have to beg on the highway."

"Try anyway," said the boy.

"Well, we can try, but it's not likely that anyone will even answer our knock at the door."

The girls walked up to the house and knocked on the front door. The master of the house was standing by the fire thinking about the horse when he heard the knocking. He went to see who was at the door, telling himself not to be tempted into letting anyone in. As he fumbled the lock, a gust of wind came along, wrenched the door from his hand and swung it open. To close it, he had to step out on the porch. When he got back into the house, the two little girls were already standing inside. They were two beggar girls, ragged, dirty and starving—two little children bent under the burden of beggar's packs almost as big as they were.

"Why are you out prowling at this hour of the night?" asked the master gruffly. The two children did not answer right away. They took off their packs. Then they stretched out their tiny hands in greeting. "We are Anna and Britta Maja from Engård," said the older of the two, "and we were going to ask for shelter for tonight."

The man ignored their friendly greeting and was about to

drive them away when he remembered something. "Engård—wasn't that a little cabin where a poor widow with five children lived?" he wondered. The widow had owed his father a few hundred kroner, and to get back his money he had sold her cabin. After that the widow and her three oldest children went to Norrland to look for employment. The two youngest became charges of the parish.

As he called this to mind, he grew bitter. He knew that his father had been criticized for squeezing out the money, but it belonged to him. "What are you doing?" he asked crossly. "The board of charities took charge of you, so why do you roam around and beg?"

"It is not our fault," the older girl replied. "The people with whom we are living have sent us out to beg."

"Well, your packs are full, so you can't complain. Eat whatever you have with you. You won't get any food here; all the women have gone to bed. Then lie down in the corner by the hearth. At least you won't freeze tonight."

He waved his hand as if to ward them off, and his eyes took on a hard look. He was thankful that his father had taken care of his property. Otherwise he might have been forced in childhood to run about and beg like these children.

The howling wind mocked him again. How strange, he thought, that when the wind repeated his thoughts, they seemed so stupid, hard, and false.

Meanwhile, the children sat on the floor, whispering.

"Be quiet," he growled. He was in such an irritable mood that he could have beaten them.

The children still whispered, and once again he told them to be quiet.

"When Mother went away," piped a little voice, "she made me promise that every night I would say my evening prayer. I must do this for Mother's sake. Britta Maja must, too. As soon as we have said 'God who cares for little children—' we will be quiet."

The master sat quite still while the children said their prayers. Then he rose and paced back and forth, back and forth, wringing his hands.

"The horse driven out and ruined, these two children turned into road beggars—both Father's doings. Perhaps he was wrong after all."

He sat down again and held his head in his hands. His lips quivered. Tears welled in his eyes, and he hastily wiped them away. More tears came; he could not stop them.

When his mother entered the room, he swung his chair around, turning his back to her. She must have noticed something unusual, because she stood behind him a long time as if waiting for him to turn around and talk to her. She knew how hard it was for men to talk of things they felt most deeply.

From her bedroom she had seen everything that had taken place in the living room. She walked very carefully over to the two sleeping children, so as not to waken them. She lifted them and carried them to her own bed. Then she returned to her son.

"Lars," she said, as if she did not see that he was weeping, "let me keep these children."

"What, Mother?" he gasped, trying to smother his sobs.

"I have been suffering for years—ever since Father took the cabin from their mother, and so have you."

"Yes, but—"

"I want to keep them here and make something of them. They are too good to beg."

He could not speak, for now the tears were beyond his control. He took his old mother's wrinkled hand and patted it.

Then he jumped up as if something had frightened him.

"What would Father have said?"

"Father had his day at ruling," retorted the mother. "This is your day. As long as Father lived, we had to obey him. Now is your opportunity to show what you are."

Her son was so atonished that he stopped crying.

"I have already shown what I am."

"No, you haven't," protested his mother. "You have only imitated him. Father went through hard times that made him afraid of poverty. He believed that he had to think of himself before anyone else. You have never known hard times. You have more than you need, and it would be unnatural if you did not think of others."

Back when the two little girls entered the house, Nils had slipped in behind them and hidden in a dark corner. He hadn't been there long before he saw the shine of the shed key, which the farmer had thrust into his coat pocket.

"When the master of the house drives the children out, I will take the key and run," he thought.

But the children were not driven out, and the boy crouched in the corner, not knowing what to do next.

The mother and her son talked for a long time. Gradually his features relaxed, and he looked like another person. All the while, he was stroking the wrinkled old hand.

"Now we may as well retire," said the old lady when she was sure that he was calm.

"No," he said, rising, "I cannot go to bed yet. There's a stranger outside. I must offer him shelter tonight."

He drew on his coat, lit a lantern, and went out. There were the same wind and chill, but he began to sing softly. He wondered if the horse would remember him and if he would be glad to come back to his old stable.

As Lars crossed the house yard, he heard a door slam.

"The shed door has blown open again," he thought, and went over to close it.

A moment later he stood by the shed and was just going to shut the door, when he heard a rustling sound.

The boy, who had been watching for an opportunity, had run to the shed where he had left the animals, but they were no longer waiting out in the rain. A strong wind had long since thrown open the door and they were inside.

What Lars had heard was Nils running into the shed. By the light of the lantern, the man could see that the whole floor was covered with sleeping cattle. There was no human being to be seen. The animals weren't tied, either.

He was enraged at the intrusion and began shouting to rouse the sleepers and drive them out, but the animals refused to be disturbed. The only one that rose was an old horse that came slowly toward him.

Lars became silent. He knew the animal by its gait. He raised the lantern, and the horse came over to him. Lars stroked and patted the old head resting on his shoulder.

"My old horsy, my old horsy," he said. "What have they done to you? Yes, my old friend, I will buy you back. You will never again have to leave this place. You shall do whatever you like, horsy mine. The animals you have brought here may stay here for the night, but you shall come with me to the stable. Now I can give you all the oats you can eat, and I won't have to smuggle them. You're not all used up, either. The handsomest horse on the church knoll—that's what you will be once more. There, there. There, there."

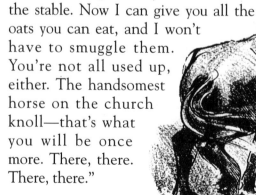

Chapter Three

The Breaking up of the Ice

Thursday, April twenty-eighth.

······················

The next day the weather was clear and beautiful. People were thankful for the strong west wind that had swept in, because it was drying up the rain-soaked roads.

Early in the morning, the two Småland children, Osa the goose girl and little Mats, were walking on the highway leading from Sörmland to Närke. The road ran along the southern shore of Hjälmar Lake, and the children were looking at the ice, which covered most of the lake.

The morning sun sparkled on the ice, making it bright and tempting. As far as Osa and little Mats could see, the ice was firm and dry. The rain had run down into cracks and hollows, or been absorbed by the ice itself. The children saw only the sound ice.

They were on their way north, and they couldn't help thinking of all the steps they would save by cutting across the lake instead of going around it. They knew, to be sure, that spring ice was dangerous, but this looked safe. They could see that it was several inches thick near the shore. They even saw a path to follow, and the opposite shore seemed so near that they ought to be able to get there in an hour.

"Let's cross it," begged little Mats. "If we're careful, we can do it."

So they went out on the lake. The ice was fairly easy to walk on, although there was more water on it than they had expected, and here and there were cracks where the water sprung up. They had to watch for such places, but it was easy enough with the sun shining.

The children made good time, and they talked about how smart they were to have gone out on the ice instead of hiking on the slushy road.

After awhile they came to Vin Island, where an old woman had seen them from her window. She rushed from her cabin, waved and shouted something which they couldn't hear. They knew that she was warning them not to go any farther, but they could not see any danger. They went on past Vin Island and had a stretch of seven miles of ice ahead of them.

Out there was so much water that the children had to take roundabout ways, but they thought it only a game. They tried to see which of them could find the soundest ice. They were neither tired nor hungry, and the whole day was ahead of them, and they laughed at every obstacle they met.

Now and then they looked toward their destination. The shore still appeared far away, although they had been walking more than an hour.

"The shore seems to be moving away from us," little Mats said, beginning to worry.

The wind was becoming stronger every minute, pressing against them so they could hardly go on. Most amazing of all was the loud roar. Where did it come from? They had walked to the west of the big island, Valen, and they thought they were nearing the north shore. Suddenly the wind picked up, and the roar grew even louder. Now they were uneasy.

All at once it occurred to them that the roar was caused by the foaming and rushing of the waves breaking against a shore. Even this seemed improbable since the lake was still covered with ice.

They looked around. Far in the west was a white bank stretching clear across the lake. They thought at first that it was a snowbank along a road, but before long they realized that it was foam-capped waves dashing against the ice.

Osa and little Mats held hands and ran without saying a word. Open sea lay beyond in the west, and suddenly the streak of foam appeared to be moving east.

The ice under their feet rose and sank as if someone from below were pushing it. They heard a hollow boom, and then there were cracks in the ice all around them. The next moment all was still, then the rising and sinking began again. The cracks widened into crevices through which the water bubbled. The crevices became gaps. Soon the ice was divided into large floes.

"Osa," said little Mats, "the ice is breaking up."

"Run for your life!" his sister shouted.

There was some hard and sound ice left, which formed large, unbroken surfaces. The greatest danger for the children lay in the fact that they could not look down from the air to see which ice was safe, so they wandered back and forth, going farther out on the lake instead of nearer land.

At last, confused and terrified, they stood still and cried.

A flock of wild geese flew by. They shrieked and cackled, but above all the noise, the children could hear an almost-human voice: "Go to the right, the right, the right!" They tried to follow the advice, but before long they were again facing a broad gap in the ice.

They heard the geese shrieking above them, and amid the cackle, they distinguished the words, "Stay where you are! Stay where you are!"

The children stood still. In a few minutes, the ice floes floated together so that they could cross the gap. Then they began to run. They were afraid not only of the danger, but of the mysterious help.

When they had to stop, they heard the voice again: "Straight ahead, straight ahead!"

In half an hour they had reached Ljunger Point, where they left the ice and waded to shore. They were still terribly frightened, even though they were on firm land. They did not stop to look back at the lake, where the waves were pitching the ice floes faster and faster, but ran on. Osa paused suddenly.

"Wait, little Mats. I have forgotten something."

Osa went back to the strand, where she stopped. There she placed a little wooden shoe on a stone where it could be plainly seen. Without looking back, she returned to her little brother.

The instant her back was turned, a big white goose shot down from the sky like a streak of lightning, snatched the wooden shoe, and flew away with it.

THE TRAVELS OF
BOOK TWO
NILS HOLGERSSON

Chapter Four

Thumbietot and the Bears

The Ironworks
....

Thursday, April twenty-eighth.

After the wild geese and Thumbietot helped Osa and little Mats across the ice, they flew into Västmanland, where they landed in a grain field to feed and rest.

A strong west wind blew almost the whole day on which the geese traveled over the mining districts, and as soon as they attempted to direct their course north they were blown toward the east.

Akka thought that Smirre Fox was in the eastern part of the province, so she would not fly in that direction. She turned back again and again, struggling west with great difficulty. At this rate the geese advanced very slowly, and late in the afternoon they were still in the Västmanland mining districts.

Toward evening the wind decreased, and the tired travelers hoped that they would have an interval of easy flight before sundown. Then along came a violent gust of wind that tossed the geese before it as if they were balls. The boy, who had been sitting comfortably, was lifted from the goose's back and hurled into space.

Little and light as he was, he could not fall straight to the ground in such a wind; so at first he was carried along with it, drifting down slowly, as a leaf falls from a tree.

"This isn't so bad," thought the boy as he fell. "I'm tumbling as easily as if I were a scrap of paper. Morton Goosey-Gander will probably hurry along and pick me up."

The first thing the boy did when he landed was to wave his cap so that the white gander could see where he was.

"Here am I. Where are you? Here am I. Where are you?" he called and was surprised that Morton Goosey-Gander was not already at his side. The big white gander was not to be seen, nor was the wild goose flock outlined against the sky. It had disappeared.

Nils thought this was odd, but he was not frightened. Not for a second did it occur to him that Akka and Morton Goosey-Gander would abandon him. No doubt the unexpected gust of wind had borne them along with it. As soon as they could turn, they would come back for him.

"But where am I?" he wondered.

He had been watching the sky for some time. Now he looked around. Apparently he had dropped into a deep, wide mountain cave. It was as big as a church, with almost straight up-and-down walls on all four sides and no roof at all. On the ground were huge rocks among which moss and brush and dwarfed birches grew. Here and there in the wall were projections from which hung rickety ladders. At one side there was a dark passage, which must have led deep into the mountain.

"Oh, no! This is an abandoned mine. If I don't get out of here, the geese will never find me."

He was about to go over to the wall when someone seized him from behind, and he heard a gruff voice growl in his ear, "Who are you?"

The boy turned, and in the confusion of the moment he thought he was facing a huge rock covered with brown moss. Then he saw that the rock had broad paws, a head, two eyes and a growling mouth.

The animal knocked him down before he could answer,

rolled him back and forth, and nuzzled him. It was about ready to eat him when it seemed to change its mind.

"Brumme and Mulle... Come here, cubs. I have something good for you to eat."

A pair of frowzy cubs, as uncertain on their feet and as woolly as puppies, came tumbling along.

"What have you got, Mama Bear? May we see? May we see?" shrieked the cubs excitedly.

"Bears! I guess Smirre Fox won't need to chase me anymore," thought the boy.

The mother bear pushed him toward her cubs. One of them nabbed him and ran off with him, but the cub did not bite hard. He was playful and wanted to amuse himself with Thumbietot before eating him. The other cub wanted to get the boy away for himself, and as he lumbered along he fell onto the first. The two cubs rolled over each other, biting, clawing, and snarling.

Nils got loose, ran to the wall, and started to climb it. Both cubs scurried after him, caught up and tossed him down on the moss.

"Now I know what a little mouse goes through when it falls into a cat's claws," thought the boy.

He made several attempts to get away. He ran down the old tunnel and hid behind the rocks, but the cubs hunted him out, go where he would. The instant they caught him, they let him go so that he could run away again and they could recapture him. At last the boy collapsed on the ground.

"Run," growled the cubs, "or we will eat you."

"Eat me, then," said the boy. "I'm tired."

The cubs rushed back to their mother and complained, "Mama, he won't play anymore."

"Then divide him evenly between you," said Mother Bear.

When Nils heard her, he got up and began to run again.

At bedtime, the mother bear called to her cubs, "Come now. Cuddle up to me and go to sleep."

The cubs had had such a good time with Thumbietot that they laid him between them and put their paws over him; they didn't want him to move without waking them. The bear cubs went right to sleep. Nils thought that now at last he could escape, but he was so tired that he too fell asleep.

After awhile, Father Bear came climbing down the mountain wall. The boy was wakened by the bear tearing away stone and gravel as he swung himself into the old mine. Nils was afraid to move much, but he managed to stretch and turn over so that he could see the big bear. He was an awfully coarse, huge old animal, with enormous paws, glistening tusks, and wicked little eyes. The boy shuddered as he stared at this monarch of the forest.

"It smells like a human being around here," said Father Bear the instant he came up to Mother Bear, and his growling was like rolling thunder.

"How could you imagine anything so ridiculous?" responded Mother Bear without disturbing herself. "If a human *had* come in here by our cubs, there wouldn't be enough left of him for you to catch his scent."

Father Bear lay down beside her and the cubs.

"Don't worry about anything," the mother bear went on. "Now tell me what you have been doing. I haven't seen you for a week."

"I've been looking for a different place for us to live," said Father Bear. "I visited our relatives at Ekshärad, thinking there might be room for us there. Not one bear's den was left in the forest."

"Humans want the whole earth to themselves," said Mother Bear. "Even if we leave them and their cattle alone and eat only lichens, insects and green plants, we can't live without being disturbed. Where can we go to live in peace?"

"We were comfortable here for many years," replied her mate, "until people built the noise shop in our neighborhood. Lately I have been thinking about the land east of Dal River, over by Garpen Mountain. Old mine pits are plentiful there, as well as other retreats where we might be safe from people—"

Father Bear sat up and sniffed. "It's strange how I catch that odd human scent every time I talk about people."

"Go look for yourself," challenged Mother Bear. "Where could a human being hide here?"

The bear nosed around the cave. Finally he returned and lay down without another word.

"What did I tell you?" said Mother Bear. "But of course you think your nose and ears are better than mine."

"One can't be too careful," said Father Bear gently. Then he leaped up with a roar. As luck would have it, one of the cubs had moved a paw over Nils' face, and the boy sneezed. Father Bear knocked the cubs to the right and left and discovered Nils before he had time to get up. He would have swallowed the boy if Mother Bear had not pushed herself between them.

"Don't touch him. He belongs to the cubs," she said. "They had such fun with him the whole evening that they couldn't bear to eat him. They're saving him for breakfast."

"You don't understand!" Father Bear roared. "Can't you scent his human odor? If I don't eat him, he will harm us."

He opened his jaws again; but meanwhile, the boy had had

time to think. He dug into his knapsack and pulled out some matches, his only weapon of defense. He struck one on his leather breeches and stuck the burning match into the bear's open mouth.

Father Bear snorted when he smelled the sulphur, and the flame went out. Nils was ready to light another, but curiously, the bear did not repeat the attack.

"Can you light many of those little blue roses?" Father Bear asked.

"Sure, I can," Nils boasted.

"Good!" exclaimed the bear. "Then you can help me. I'm glad I didn't eat you."

Father Bear clamped his jaws around him and climbed out of the mining pit. He did this with remarkable ease, considering that he was so big and heavy. As soon as he was up, he made for the woods. Obviously he was created to squeeze through dense forests. The heavy bear pushed through the brushwood like a boat through water.

Father Bear ran along until he reached a hill at the edge of the forest, where he could see the noise shop. He lay down and placed the boy in front of him, holding him securely between his forepaws.

"Look at the noise shop," he commanded. The massive ironworks stood at the edge of a waterfall. Dark clouds of smoke rose from high chimneys, blasting furnaces were blazing, and light shone from all the windows. Inside, hammers and rolling mills were going with such force that the air rang with their clatter and boom. All around the work- shops were immense coal sheds, great slag heaps, ware- houses, wood- piles and

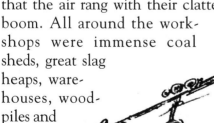

toolsheds. Just beyond were long rows of laborers' homes, pretty villas, schoolhouses, meeting halls and shops. All was quiet, and apparently everyone was asleep.

Nils gazed intently at the ironworks. The earth around them was black. The sky above them was like an enormous fiery dome. The rapids, white with foam, rushed by them. The buildings themselves were sending out light and smoke, fire and sparks. It was the grandest spectacle the boy had ever seen.

"Do you think you could set fire to a place like that?" asked the bear doubtfully.

Wedged between the bear's paws, Nils was thinking that the only thing that would save him was the bear's high opinion of what he could do. "Big or little," he replied, "I can burn it down."

"Let me tell you something," said Father Bear. "My forefathers lived in this region from the time that the forests first sprang up. From them I inherited hunting grounds and pastures, lairs and retreats, and have lived here in peace all of my life. In the beginning I wasn't bothered by the humans. They dug in the mountains and picked up a little ore down here, by the rapids. They had a forge and a furnace, but the hammers pounded only a few hours during the day, and the furnace wasn't fired more than once every two moons.

"It wasn't so bad then; but these last years, since people built this noise shop, which keeps up the racket day and night, life has become intolerable. Just a manager and a couple of black-smiths used to live here, but now there are so many people that I can never feel safe from them. I thought that I would have to move away, but I think I have just discovered a better alternative."

The boy wondered what the alternative was, but he didn't have time to ask before Father Bear took him in his mouth again and lumbered down the hill. Nils couldn't see, but by the increasing noise he knew they were approaching the rolling mills.

Father Bear was well informed about the ironworks. He had prowled around there on many a dark night, had observed what had gone on within, and had wondered if there would never be an end to the work. He had tested the walls with his paws and wished that he were strong enough to knock down the whole structure with a single blow.

He wasn't easily distinguishable against the dark ground; and in the shadow of the walls, there was not much danger of his being seen. He walked fearlessly among the workshops and climbed to the top of a slag heap. There he sat up on his haunches, took the boy between his forepaws and held him up.

"Look into the building," he commanded. A strong current of air was being forced into a big cylinder which was suspended from the ceiling and filled with molten iron. As this current rushed into the hot iron, showers of sparks of all colors spurted up in bunches and sprays and long clusters. They struck against the wall and came splashing down over the whole room. Father Bear let the boy watch the gorgeous spectacle until the blowing was over and the flowing and sparkling red steel had been poured into ingot molds. Nils was fascinated by the marvelous display and almost forgot that he was held captive between a bear's paws.

Father Bear let him look into the rolling mill, too. He saw a workman take a short, thick bar of iron at white heat from a furnace opening and place it under a roller. When the iron came out from under the roller, it was flattened and extended. Another workman seized it and shoved it beneath a heavier roller, which made it still longer and thinner. The iron was passed from roller to roller, squeezed and drawn out until, finally, it curled along the floor like a long, red thread.

While the first bar of iron was being pressed, a second was taken from the furnace and placed under the rollers. Then a third was brought from the furnace. Fresh threads came crawling over the floor like hissing snakes. The boy was dazzled by the iron, but he found it even more interesting to watch the workmen who, dexterously and delicately, seized the glowing snakes with their tongs and forced them under the rollers. Handling the hissing iron seemed like play for them.

"That's real man's work." the boy thought to himself.

The bear let the boy have a look at the furnace and the forge as well, and Nils became more and more astonished as he saw how the blacksmiths handled iron and fire.

"Those men have no fear of heat and flames," he thought. The men were sooty and grimy. He imagined that they were some sort of firefolk, and that was why they could bend and mold the iron any way they wanted to. How could ordinary men have such power?

"They keep this up day after day, night after night," said Father Bear, as he dropped wearily to the ground. "You can understand how tiresome it has become. I'm mighty glad that at last I can put a stop to it."

"How will you do that?" asked the boy.

"You are going to set fire to the building—that's how," said Father Bear. "That would put an end to all this work, and I could remain in my old home."

The boy shivered from head to toe. So this was why Father Bear had brought him here.

"If you promise to set fire to the ironworks, I will spare your life," the bear said. "But if you don't—"

The huge workshops were brick, and the boy was thinking that no matter how much Father Bear threatened, it would be impossible to obey him. Or was it? Just beyond them lay a pile of woodchips and shavings that could easily be set on fire, and beside the woodchips was a woodpile that almost reached the woodshed. The coal shed extended to the workshops, and if that caught on fire, the flames would fly over to the roof of the iron foundry. Everything combustible would burn. The walls would fall from the heat, and the machinery would be destroyed.

"Will you or won't you?" Father Bear demanded.

The boy knew that he should say no, but he also knew that the bear's paws would squeeze him to death if he did.

"I need time to think it over," he said.

"Very well," said Father Bear, "but iron is what has given people the advantage over us bears, which is another good reason for my wanting to stop the work here."

Nils had hoped to figure out an escape plan, but instead he began to think of the benefits of iron. People needed iron for nearly everything. There was iron in the plow that broke up the field, in the axe that felled the trees for building houses, in the scythe that mowed the grain, and in the knife, which had many uses. There was iron in the horse's bit, in the lock on the door, in the nails that held furniture together, in the sheathing that covered the roof. The rifle that drove away wild animals was made of iron, also the pick that had broken up the mine. Iron covered the men-of-war he had seen at Karlskrona. Trains steamed through the country on iron rails. The needle that had stitched his coat was of iron. The shears that clipped the sheep and the kettle that cooked the food were iron. Big and little alike—much that was indispensable was made from iron. Father Bear was perfectly right in saying that iron had given people their mastery over the bears.

"Now will you or won't you?" Father Bear repeated.

The boy was startled. He still hadn't thought of a way to save himself.

"Be patient," he said. "This is a serious matter for me, and I have to have time to think."

"Well then, think for another moment," said Father Bear. "But let me tell you that it's because of iron that people have become so much wiser than we bears are. For this alone, if for nothing else, I would like to stop the work here."

Again the boy tried to plan his escape, but all he could think about was the iron and how much thinking people must have done before they discovered how to produce iron from ore. He imagined sooty blacksmiths of old bending over the forge, pondering how to handle it properly. Perhaps it was because they had thought so much about iron that intelligence had been developed until finally people were able to build great works like these. The fact was that people owed more to the iron than they realized.

"Well, what do you have to say? Will you burn down the ironworks?" insisted Father Bear.

The boy shrank back. "It's not as easy as you think," he said.

"I can wait for you a little longer," said Father Bear, "but after that you won't have another chance. It's the fault of the iron that people can live here on the property of the bears, and I want the ironworks destroyed."

Anxious as he was, the boy could only think of what he had seen when he flew over the mining districts. It was strange that there should be so much activity and work in this wilderness area.

"Just think how poor and desolate this place would be if it weren't for iron.

"This foundry has provided employment for people and brought in railways and telegraph wires and—"

"I'm still waiting," growled the bear. "Will you or won't you?"

The boy wiped his forehead. The iron was useful to both rich and poor, and it had provided bread for many people in this land.

"I won't!" he shouted.

Father Bear squeezed him a little harder, but said nothing.

"You won't get me to destroy the ironworks," defied the boy. "The iron has been too great a blessing to harm it."

"Then you don't expect to live long, do you?" asked the bear softly.

"No, I don't expect to," returned the boy.

Father Bear gripped him still harder. Tears fell from the boy's eyes, but he did not cry out.

"Very well, then," said Father Bear, slowly raising his paw, hoping that the boy would give in at the last moment.

Then the boy heard something click and saw the muzzle of a rifle two paces away.

"Don't you hear the clicking of a trigger?" shouted the boy. "Run, or you'll be shot!"

Father Bear ran, and he took the boy with him. As he ran, a couple of shots sounded, and the bullets grazed his ears; but, luckily, he escaped.

The boy thought, as he was dangling from the bear's mouth, that he had never been as stupid as he was tonight. If he had kept quiet, the bear would have been shot and he would have been free. But he had become so accustomed to helping animals that he did it naturally, as a matter of course.

After Father Bear had gone some distance into the woods, he paused and set the boy down on the ground.

"Thank you, little one," he said. "The bullets would have caught me if you hadn't warned me. I owe you something for that act of kindness. If you ever meet another bear, tell him this—I'll whisper it to you—and the bear won't touch you." Father Bear whispered a word or two into the boy's ear and hurried away; he thought he heard hounds and hunters pursuing him.

Nils was in the forest, free and unharmed, and he could hardly understand how it was possible.

The wild geese had been flying back and forth the whole evening, looking and calling, but they had been unable to find Thumbietot. They searched long after the sun had set, and finally, when it had grown so dark that they were forced to alight somewhere for the night, they were downhearted.

They thought the boy had been killed in the fall and was lying dead in the forest, where they could not see him.

But the next morning, when the sun peeped over the hills and awakened the wild geese, the boy lay sleeping, as usual, in their midst. When he woke and heard them shrieking and cackling their astonishment, he could not help laughing.

They were so eager to know what had happened to him that they refused to go to breakfast until they had heard the whole story. Nils told them most of it, but he seemed reluctant to tell them all of it. "Maybe you already know how I got back to you," he said.

"No. We thought you were killed."

"Well, you see, when Father Bear left me, I climbed up into a pine and fell asleep. At daybreak I was awakened by an eagle hovering over me. He picked me up with his talons and carried me away. He didn't hurt me, but flew straight here to you and dropped me down among you."

"Didn't he tell you who he was?" asked the big white gander.

"He was gone before I had time to thank him. I thought that Mother Akka had sent him after me."

"That's strange," remarked the white goosey-gander. "Are you sure it was an eagle?"

"No," admitted the boy, "but he was so big and splendid that he couldn't have been anything else."

Morton Goosey-Gander turned to the wild geese to get their opinion, but they stood gazing into the air as though they were thinking of something else.

"Let's go eat breakfast," said Akka, quickly spreading her wings.

Chapter Five

The Flood

The Swans

May first to fourth.

A thunderstorm raged in the district north of Lake Mälaren, lasting several days. The sky was a dull gray, the wind whistled, and the rain beat down. Both people and animals knew the spring could not be ushered in any other way, but that thought didn't make the bad weather any more bearable.

After it had been raining for a whole day, the snowdrifts in the pine forests began to melt in earnest, and the spring brooks grew lively. All the pools on the farms, the standing water in the ditches, the water that oozed between the tufts in marshes and swamps—all were in motion and tried to find their way to creeks and be borne along to the sea. The creeks rushed as fast as possible down to the rivers, and the rivers did their utmost to carry the water to Lake Mälaren.

All the lakes and rivers in Uppland and the mining district threw off their ice covers on one and the same day so that the creeks were full of ice floes, which rose clear up to their banks. Swollen as they were, they emptied into Lake Mälaren, and it was not long before the lake had taken in as much water as it could hold.

Down by the outlet was a raging torrent. Norrström is a narrow channel, and it could not let out the water quickly enough. Besides, there was a strong easterly wind that lashed against the land, obstructing the stream when it tried to carry the fresh water into the East Sea. Since the rivers kept running to Mälaren with more water than it could dispose of, there was nothing for the big lake to do but overflow its banks.

It rose slowly, as if reluctant to injure its beautiful shores, but because they were mostly low and gradually sloping, the water flooded several acres of land. That was enough to create great alarm.

Lake Mälaren is unique, being made up of a succession of narrow fjords, bays and inlets. Nowhere does it spread into a storm center, but seems to have been created solely for pleasure boating, yachting tours and fishing. Nowhere does it present bar-

ren, desolate, wind-swept shores. It looks as if it would never expect its edges to hold anything except country seats, summer villas, manors and amusement resorts. Just because Lake Mälaren usually presents a friendly appearance, there is all the more havoc when it drops its smiling expression in the spring and shows that it can be serious.

The Flood

At that critical time Smirre Fox happened to prowl through a birch grove just north of Lake Mälaren. As usual, he was thinking about Thumbietot and the wild geese, and wondering how to find them. He had lost all track.

As he stole cautiously along, more discouraged than usual, he caught sight of Agar, the carrier pigeon, who had perched on a birch branch.

"Agar! What luck to find you," exclaimed Smirre. "Maybe you can tell me where Akka from Kebnekaise and her flock are these days."

"Maybe I do know where they are," Agar teased, "but I'm not likely to tell you."

"Please yourself," retorted Smirre. "You can still take a message that I have for them. You know the condition of Lake Mälaren, don't you? It's flooding, and the swans who live in Hjälsta Bay are about to see their nests and all their eggs destroyed.

Daylight, the king of the swans, has heard of the tomten who travels with the wild geese and has the solution to every problem. He has sent me to ask Akka to bring Thumbietot to Hjälsta Bay."

"I suppose I can convey your message," Agar replied, "but I don't understand how the little boy could help the swans."

"I don't either," said Smirre, "but he can do almost anything, it seems."

"It surprises me that Daylight would send his message by a fox," Agar remarked.

"We're not exactly what you would call good friends," said Smirre smoothly, "but in an emergency like this we must help each other. Perhaps it would be just as well not to tell Akka that you got the message from a fox. Between you and me, Akka's inclined to be suspicious."

........................◆........................

The safest refuge for waterfowl in the whole Mälaren district is Hjälsta Bay. It has low shores, shallow water and is covered with reeds.

By no means as large as Lake Tåkern, Hjälsta is nonetheless a good retreat for birds since it has long been forbidden territory to hunters. It is the home of a great many swans. To protect them, the owner of the old castle nearby has prohibited all shooting on the bay.

As soon as Akka received word that the swans needed her help, she and her flock swiftly flew down to Hjälsta Bay. The

evening they arrived, they saw at a glance that there had been a great disaster. The swans' nests had been torn away, and the wind was driving them down the bay. Some had already fallen apart, two or three had capsized, and the eggs lay at the bottom of the lake.

When Akka alighted on the bay, all the swans living there were gathered near the eastern shore, where they were protected from the wind. Although they had suffered because of the flooding, they would not show it.

"It is useless to cry," they said. "With all the root fibers and stems here, we can build new nests." None had thought of asking a stranger to help them, and the swans had no idea that Smirre Fox had sent for the wild geese.

Several hundred swans were resting on the water, all in order, according to rank and station. The young and inexperienced were farthest out, the old and wise closer to the middle of the group, and right in the center sat Daylight, the swan king, and Snow White, the swan queen, who were older than any of the others and regarded the rest of the swans as their children.

The geese had landed on the western shore of the bay. When Akka saw where the swans were, she immediately swam toward them. She hadn't expected to be summoned, but she considered it an honor. As Akka approached the swans, she paused to see if the geese who followed her swam in a straight line and at even distances apart.

"Swim quickly," she ordered. "Don't stare at the swans as if you had never seen anything so beautiful, and don't mind what they may say to you."

This was not the first time that Akka had called on the aristocratic swans. They had always received her in a manner befitting a renowned traveler like herself, yet she did not like the idea of swimming among them. She never felt so gray and insignificant as when she met swans. One or another of them was sure to drop a remark about "common gray feathers" and "poor folk."

This time everything passed off unusually well. The swans politely made way for the wild geese, who swam forward through a kind of passageway, which formed an avenue bordered by shimmering, white birds.

It was a magnificent sight. The swans spread their wings like sails to impress the strangers, and they refrained from making comments. Akka was surprised. Evidently Daylight had noted the swans' misbehavior in the past and had told them to conduct themselves in a proper manner—so thought Akka.

Just as the swans were making an effort to observe the rules of etiquette, they saw the goosey-gander, who swam last in the long goose line. Then there was a murmur of disapproval, even of threats, among the swans.

"What's this?" shouted one. "Do the wild geese intend to dress up in white feathers?"

"Do they think that makes swans of them?" cried another.

They began shrieking—some louder than others—in their strong, resonant voices. It was impossible to explain that a tame goosey-gander had come with the wild geese.

"That must be the goose king himself," they taunted. "There's no limit to their audacity."

"That's no goose. It's a tame duck!"

The big white gander obeyed Akka's admonition to pay no attention, no matter what he might hear. He kept quiet and swam as fast as he could, but it was no use. The swans became even ruder.

"What kind of frog is he carrying on his back?" asked one. "They must think we can't tell it's a frog because it's dressed like a human being."

The swans, who had been resting in perfect order, swam around excitedly. They crowded forward to get a glimpse of the wild white goose.

"That white goosey-gander ought to be ashamed to come here and parade in front of swans."

"He's probably just as gray as the rest of them. He must have gotten into a flour barrel at some farmhouse."

The Flood

Akka was about to ask Daylight what kind of help he wanted, when the swan king noticed the uproar among the swans.

"What do I see? Haven't I told you to be polite to strangers?" he said with a frown.

Snow White, the swan queen, swam out to restore order among her subjects, and again Daylight turned to Akka.

Soon Snow White returned, and she was disturbed.

"Can't you keep them quiet?" Daylight shouted in the din.

"There's a white wild goose over there," answered Snow White. Isn't it shameful? No wonder they're furious."

"A white wild goose?" scoffed Daylight. "That's ridiculous! There can't be such a thing. You must be mistaken."

The crowd around Morton Goosey-Gander grew larger and larger. Akka and the other wild geese tried to swim to him, but were jostled back and forth. The old swan king, who was the strongest among them, pushed all the others aside and made his way to the goosey-gander. When he saw that there really was a white goose on the water, he was as indignant as the rest. Hissing with rage, he flew straight at the goose and tore out feathers.

"I'll teach you a lesson, wild goose," he shrieked, "so that you won't come here dressed in white."

"Fly, Morton Goosey-Gander! Fly, fly!" cried Akka. She knew that the swans would pull out every feather the goosey-gander had.

"Fly, fly!" screamed Thumbietot, too.

But the goosey-gander was so hedged in by the swans that he didn't have space to spread his wings. All around him the swans stretched out their long necks, opened their strong bills, and plucked his feathers.

Morton Goosey-Gander defended himself by striking and biting. The wild geese also began to fight the swans. It was obvious how this would have ended had not the geese received unexpected help.

A redtail saw that they were being roughly treated by the swans. Instantly he made the shrill call that little birds use when they need help to drive off a hawk or a falcon. Three calls had barely sounded when all the little birds in the vicinity came shooting to Hjälsta Bay, as if on wings of lightning.

The delicate little creatures swooped down on the swans, screeched in their ears, and obstructed their view with the flutter of their tiny wings. They made them dizzy with their fluttering and drove them to distraction with their cries of "Shame, shame, swans!"

The attack of the small birds lasted but a moment. When they were gone and the swans came to their senses, the geese were already at the other end of the bay.

The New Watchdog

At least this much could be said in the swans' favor—when they saw that the wild geese had escaped, they were too proud to chase them. Fortunately the geese could stand on a clump of reeds in perfect comfort and sleep.

Nils Holgersson was too hungry to sleep. "I have to get something to eat," he said.

In the flood season, all kinds of things were floating on the water, so it was not difficult for a little boy like Nils to find a craft. He hopped down on a small stump that had drifted in among the reeds. Then he picked up a stick and began to pole toward shore.

When he reached land, he heard a splash in the water. First he saw a lady swan asleep in her big nest close to him. Then he saw that a fox had taken a few steps into the water and was sneaking up to the swan's nest.

"Hey, hey, hey! Get up, get up!" cried the boy, beating the water with his stick.

The lady swan rose, but not quickly enough to prevent the fox from pouncing on her if he'd wanted to. Instead, the fox went after the boy.

Thumbietot saw the fox coming and ran for his life. Wide stretches of meadow lay before him. He couldn't see a tree to climb or a hole to hide in. He had to keep running.

The boy was a good runner, but it stands to reason that he

could not win a race with a fox. Not far from the bay there were a number of little cabins, with candle lights shining through the windows. Naturally the boy ran in that direction, but he realized that long before he could reach the nearest cabin the fox would catch up to him.

Once the fox was so close that it looked as if the boy would be caught, but Nils jumped out of the way and turned back toward the bay. The fox lost time because of that maneuver. Before he could reach Nils, the boy had run up to two men who were on their way home from work.

The men were tired, and they hadn't seen either the boy or the fox, although both had been running right in front of them. The boy didn't ask for help. He was content to walk close beside them.

"The fox won't dare come near these men," he thought.

But the fox pattered up. He probably thought the men would take him for a dog.

"Whose dog can that be sneaking around here?" asked one. "He looks like he's ready to bite."

The other glanced back. "Get out of here, you," he said, and gave the fox a kick that sent it to the other side of the road. After that the fox kept at a safe distance.

The men reached a cabin and went in. Nils intended to go in with them, but when he got to the porch, he saw a big, shaggy watchdog rush out from his kennel to greet his master. Suddenly the boy changed his mind and remained out in the open.

"Watchdog, listen!" whispered the boy as soon as the men had shut the door. "Would you like to catch a fox tonight?"

The dog had poor eyesight and was cranky from being chained.

"What, I catch a fox?" he barked angrily. "Are you joking? Come within my reach and I'll teach you to make fun of me."

"I'm not afraid of you," said the boy, running up to the dog.

When the dog saw him, he was so astonished that he could not bark.

"I'm the one they call Thumbietot, who travels with the wild geese," said the boy. "Haven't you heard about me?"

"I believe the sparrows have twittered a little about you," the dog replied. "They say you've done amazing things for one your size."

"I have been rather lucky until now," the boy admitted. "But there's a fox after me. He's lying in wait for me around the corner."

"I can smell him," the dog said. "We'll soon be rid of him." The dog jumped as far as the chain would allow, barking and growling. "He won't show his face again tonight."

"It will take more than a fine bark to scare that fox," the boy replied. "He will be back...and we'll be waiting. I want you to catch him."

"Are you serious?" asked the dog.

"Come with me into your kennel. I'll tell you what to do." The boy and the watchdog went into the kennel.

Before long the fox stuck his nose out from his hiding place. He crept along cautiously. He scented the boy all the way to the kennel, but halted at a safe distance and sat down to think of a way to coax him out.

Suddenly the watchdog poked his head out and growled at him, "Go away, or I'll catch you."

"I'll sit here as long as I please," defied the fox.

"Go away," repeated the dog, "or you won't be hunting after tonight."

The fox grinned and did not move an inch. "I know how far your chain reaches," he said.

"I have warned you twice," said the dog, coming out. "Blame yourself."

Nils had unbuckled his collar, so the dog was loose. With a single bound he caught the fox. There was a struggle, but it was soon over, and the dog was the victor.

"Don't move or I'll kill you," snarled the dog. He took the fox by the scruff of his neck and pulled him to the kennel. There Nils was ready with the chain. He placed the dog collar around the fox's neck, tightening it so that he was securely chained. When he was finished, he laughed and said, "Well, Smirre, you'd better be a good watchdog."

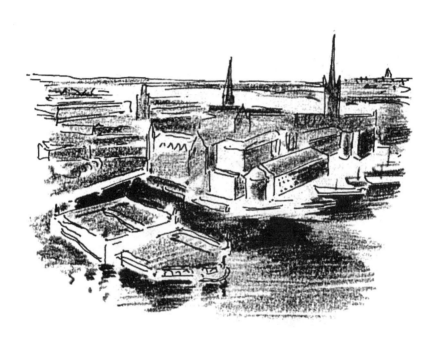

THE TRAVELS OF BOOK TWO NILS HOLGERSSON

Chapter Six

Dunfin

The City That Floats on the Water

Friday, May sixth.

No one could be more gentle and kind than the little gray goose, Dunfin. All the wild geese loved her, and the tame white goosey-gander would have died for her. When Dunfin asked for anything, not even Akka could say no.

As soon as Dunfin came to Lake Mälaren, the landscape looked familiar to her. Just beyond the lake lay the sea, with many wooded islands, and there, on a little islet, lived her parents and her brothers and sisters. She begged the wild geese to fly to her home before traveling farther north, so that she could let her family see that she was still alive; it would be such a joy to them.

Akka frankly declared that she thought Dunfin's parents and brothers and sisters had shown no great love for her when they abandoned her at Öland, but Dunfin wouldn't admit that Akka might be right.

"What else was there to do when they saw that I couldn't fly?" she protested. "I wouldn't expect them to remain in Öland for me."

Dunfin began telling the wild geese all about her home in the archipelago (an island group), to try to persuade them to make the trip. Her family lived on a rock island. Seen from a distance, it appeared to be deserted. Closer to it, one could find the choicest goose tidbits in clefts and hollows, and some of the best nesting places anywhere were hidden in the island's cliffs and osier bushes.

Best of all was the old fisherman who lived there. Dunfin had heard that when he was a young man, he had been a great marksman and had lain in the offing—far enough away from the shoreline to see but not be easily seen—and hunted birds. Now in his old age, since his wife had died and the children had left home, he had begun to care for the birds on his island. He never fired a shot at them, nor would he permit others to do so. He never disturbed the birds' nests, and when the mother birds were sitting on their eggs, he brought them food. Not one bird was afraid of him. They all loved him.

Dunfin had been in the old man's hut many times, and he had fed her bread crumbs. Because he was kind to the birds, they flocked to his island in such great numbers that it was becoming overcrowded. If one arrived a little late in the spring, all the nesting places were already occupied. That was why Dunfin's family had had to leave her behind.

Dunfin

Dunfin begged so hard that she finally had her way, although the wild geese felt that they were losing time and should be heading straight north. A little trip to the cliff island would not delay them more than a day, however, so they relented.

They started off one morning after a good breakfast and flew east over Lake Mälaren. The boy didn't know for certain where they were going, but he noticed that the farther east they flew, the livelier it was on the lake and the more built up were the shores.

Heavily freighted barges and sloops, boats and fishing smacks were on their way east, and these were met and passed by white steamers. Along the shores ran country roads and railroad tracks, and everyone was going in the same direction.

On one of the islands the boy saw a big, white castle, and to the east of it the shores were dotted with villas. At the beginning, these lay far apart. Then they came closer and closer, and finally the whole shore was lined with them. They were of every variety—here a castle, there a cottage. Then a low manor house appeared, or a mansion with many small towers. Some stood in gardens, but most of them were in the wild woods bordering the shores. In spite of their dissimilarity, they were alike in one respect—they were not plain and somber-looking like other buildings, but were brightly painted in greens and blues, reds and white, like children's playhouses.

As the boy sat on the goose's back and glanced down at the curious shore mansions, Dunfin cried out with delight: "Now I know where I am! Over there lies the City That Floats on the Water."

The boy looked ahead. At first he only saw light clouds and mists rolling over the water, but soon he caught sight of tall spires, and then houses with rows of windows. They appeared and disappeared, rolling here and there, but not a strip of shore did he see. Everything seemed to be resting on the water.

Nearer the city he saw dingy factories; not a pretty playhouse was to be seen. Heaps of coal and wood were stacked behind tall planks. Alongside black, sooty docks lay bulky freight steamers. Over all was a shimmering, transparent mist, which

made everything appear so big and strong and wonderful that it was almost beautiful.

The wild geese flew past factories and freight steamers and were nearing the cloud-enveloped spires. Suddenly all the mists sank to the water—except for the thin, fleecy ones that circled above their heads, tinted in blues and pinks. The other clouds rolled over water and land, entirely obscuring the lower portions of the houses. Only the upper stories, roofs and gables were visible. Some of the buildings appeared to be as high as the Tower of Babel. No doubt the boy knew that they were built upon hills and mountains, but he couldn't see them—only the houses that seemed to float among the white, drifting clouds. In reality the buildings were dark and dingy, for the sun in the east was not shining on them.

Nils knew that he was riding above a large city because he saw spires and house roofs rising from the clouds in every direction. Sometimes an opening was made in the circling mists, and he looked down into a swirling whirlpool. He still could not see land. All this was wonderful, but he felt distressed—as one does when happening upon something one cannot understand.

When he had gone beyond the city, he found that the ground was no longer hidden by clouds, but that shores, streams and islands were again plainly visible. He turned to see the city better, but could not; now it looked quite enchanted. The mists had taken on color from the sunshine and were rolling in the most brilliant reds, blues and yellows. The houses were white, as if built of light, and the windows and spires sparkled like fire. Everything floated on the water as before.

The geese were traveling straight east. They flew over factories and workshops, then over mansions edging the shores. Steamboats and tugs swarmed on the water, but now they came from the east and were steaming west toward the city.

The wild geese flew on, but instead of the narrow Mälaren fjords and the little islands, broader waters and larger islands spread under them. At last the land was left behind and seen no more.

They flew still farther out, where they found no more large, inhabited islands, but only numberless little rock islands scattered on the water. Now the fjords were not crowded by the land. The sea lay before them, vast and limitless.

Here the wild geese alighted on a cliff island. As soon as their feet touched the ground the boy turned to Dunfin. "What city was that?" he asked.

"I don't know what human beings have named it," said Dunfin, "but we gray geese call it the City That Floats on the Water."

The Sisters

Dunfin had two sisters—Prettywing and Goldeye. They were strong and intelligent birds, but they didn't have as soft and shiny a feather dress as Dunfin, nor did they have her sweet and gentle disposition. From the time they had been little, yellow goslings, their parents and relatives and even the old fisherman had shown them that they thought more of Dunfin than of them. The sisters had always hated her.

When the wild geese landed on the cliff island, Prettywing and Goldeye were feeding on a bit of grass close to the strand. They noticed the strangers immediately.

"See, Sister Goldeye, what fine-looking geese have come to our island," said Prettywing. "I've rarely seen such graceful birds. See that white goosey-gander with them? Did you ever set eyes on a handsomer bird? One might mistake him for a swan."

Goldeye agreed with her sister that these were certainly distinguished strangers who had come to the island. Suddenly she said, "Sister Prettywing! Oh, Sister Prettywing! Don't you see who's with them?"

When Prettywing saw Dunfin, she was so astonished that she stood for a long time with her bill wide open and only hissed. "It can't be possible! How did she get in with people of that class? We left her at Öland to freeze and starve."

"The worst of it is she will tattle to Father and Mother that we flew so close to her that we knocked her wing out of joint," said Goldeye. "You'll see. Once the story's out, we'll be driven from the island."

"I think you're right. We're in trouble now that the young one has come back," snapped Prettywing. "It would be best for us to appear as pleased as possible over her return. She's so stupid that she may not have realized that we pushed her on purpose."

While Prettywing and Goldeye were talking together, the wild geese had been standing on the strand, pluming their feathers after the flight. Now they marched in a long line up the rocky shore to the cleft where Dunfin's parents usually stopped.

Dunfin's parents were good, open-hearted geese. They had lived on the island longer than anyone else, and they counseled and helped newcomers. They too had seen the geese approach, but they had not recognized Dunfin in the flock.

"How strange to see wild geese on this island," remarked the goose master. "It's a fine flock; one can see that by their flight."

"But will there be enough food for them?" worried his goose wife, who was gentle and sweet-tempered like Dunfin.

When Akka came marching with her company, Dunfin's parents went out to meet her and welcome her to the island. Dunfin flew from her place at the end of the line and alighted between her parents.

"Mother, Father, I'm here at last!" she cried happily. When the old goose parents recognized Dunfin they were overjoyed, of course.

While the wild geese and Morton Goosey-Gander and Dunfin were chattering excitedly, trying to tell how she had been rescued, Prettywing and Goldeye came running up to them. They cried, "Welcome," and pretended to be so happy because Dunfin was home that she was deeply moved.

The wild geese fared well on the island and decided not to travel farther until the following morning. After awhile, the sisters asked Dunfin if she'd like to go with them to see where they intended to build their nests. She went along and saw that they had picked out secluded, well-protected nesting places.

"Where will you settle down, Dunfin?" they asked.

"I? Why, I don't intend to remain on the island," she said.

"I'm going with the wild geese up to Lapland."

"Oh, what a pity," said the sisters.

"I would be very happy to remain here with Father and Mother and you," said Dunfin, "if it weren't for my promise to the big, white—"

"What!" shrieked Prettywing. "Are you to have the handsome goosey-gander for your mate? Then it is—" Goldeye gave her a sharp nudge, and she stopped short.

The two cruel sisters had much to talk about all afternoon. They were furious because Dunfin had a suitor like the white goosey-gander. They had suitors too, but they were common gray geese. Since the sisters had seen Morton Goosey-Gander, they thought their own suitors so low-class that they didn't even want to look at them.

"I will grieve to death," whimpered Goldeye. "If at least it had been you, Sister Prettywing, who had captured him, I would feel better."

"I would rather see that goosey-gander dead than spend the whole summer thinking of Dunfin enjoying his company," pouted Goldeye.

The sisters were too shrewd to do other than appear friendly to Dunfin, however. In the afternoon Goldeye took Dunfin with her, so she could see the one she thought of marrying.

"He's not as attractive as the white goosey-gander," said Goldeye, "but to make up for it, I can be certain that he is what he is."

"What do you mean, Goldeye?" questioned Dunfin.

At first Goldeye would not explain what she had meant, but at last she came out with it. "We have never seen a white goose travel with wild geese," said the sister. "He's probably bewitched."

"How stupid!" retorted Dunfin indignantly. "He is a tame goose."

"He has one with him who's bewitched," said Goldeye, "and under the circumstances, he too must be bewitched. Aren't you afraid that he might actually be a black cormorant?" She was a good talker and succeeded in frightening Dunfin thoroughly.

"You don't mean what you are saying," pleaded the little gray goose. "You want to frighten me."

"I only want what is good for you, Dunfin," said Goldeye. "I can't imagine anything worse than for you to fly away with a black cormorant.

"I know what you can do to find out. Persuade him to eat some of the roots I have gathered. If he is bewitched, it will be apparent at once. If he isn't, he will stay the way he is."

The boy was sitting among the white geese, listening to Akka and the old goose master, when Dunfin came flying up to him. "Thumbietot, Thumbietot!" she cried. "Morton Goosey-Gander is dying! I have killed him!"

"Let me get up on your back, Dunfin, and take me to him." Away they flew, and Akka and the other wild geese followed them. When they got to the goosey-gander, he was prostrate on the ground. He could not utter a word, and he gasped for breath.

"Tickle him under the throat and slap him on the back," ordered Akka. The boy did so, and soon the big, white gander coughed up a large, white root that had stuck in his throat.

"Have you been eating these white roots?" asked Akka, pointing to some roots that lay on the ground.

"Yes," groaned the goosey-gander.

"It's a good thing they stuck in your throat," said Akka. "They are poisonous. If you had swallowed them, you probably would have died."

"Dunfin asked me to eat them," said the goosey-gander.

"My sister gave them to me," said Dunfin, and she told what had happened.

"Beware of your sisters, Dunfin," said Akka. "They wish you no good; depend upon it."

Dunfin couldn't believe evil of anyone. A moment later, when Prettywing asked her to come and meet her fiancé, Dunfin went along without a thought of danger.

"Oh, my beau isn't as handsome as yours," said the sister, "but he's much more courageous and daring!"

"How do you know he is?" challenged Dunfin.

"For a long time, the sea gulls and wild ducks on this island have been weeping and wailing. Every morning at daybreak a strange bird of prey comes and carries one of them off."

"What kind of bird is it?" asked Dunfin.

"I don't know," replied her sister. "His kind has never been seen here before, and he has never attacked one of us geese.

"My fiancé," Prettywing said proudly, "has made up his mind to challenge him tomorrow morning and drive him away."

"I hope he'll succeed," said Dunfin.

"I don't think he will. If he were as big and strong as your white goosey-gander, I'd be more hopeful."

"Would you like me to ask Morton Goosey-Gander to meet the strange bird?" asked Dunfin.

"Yes!" exclaimed Prettywing.

The next morning the goosey-gander was up before the sun. He stationed himself on the highest point of the island and stared in all directions. Soon he saw a big, dark bird coming from the west. The bird's wingspan was enormous, and it was easy to tell that he was an eagle.

The goosey-gander had expected to see a formidable adversary, but not an eagle. Morton could not escape with his life and he knew it, but it didn't occur to him to avoid the struggle.

The great bird swooped down on a sea gull and dug his talons into it. Before the eagle could spread his wings, Morton Goosey-Gander rushed up to him. "Drop that!" he shouted, "and don't come here again or you will have me to deal with."

"What kind of a lunatic are you?" said the eagle. "It's lucky for you I never fight with geese, or you would regret your words."

Morton Goosey-Gander thought the eagle considered himself too good to fight with him and flew at him, biting him on the throat and beating him with his wings. This, naturally, the eagle wouldn't tolerate and he began to fight, though not as hard as he could.

The boy lay sleeping in the quarters where Akka and the other wild geese slept, when Dunfin cried, "Thumbietot, Thumbietot! Morton Goosey-Gander is being torn to pieces by an eagle."

"Let me get up on your back, Dunfin, and take me to him."

When they arrived on the scene, Morton Goosey-Gander was badly wounded and bleeding, but he was still fighting. The boy shouted, "Dunfin! Call Akka and the wild geese!"

The instant he said that, the eagle stopped fighting and asked, "What did you say? Who mentioned Akka?"

He saw Thumbietot and heard the wild geese honking, so he spread his wings. "Tell Akka I never expected to run across her or any of her flock out here at sea," he said, and soared away.

"That is the eagle who once brought me back to the wild geese," the boy remarked, gazing after the bird in astonishment.

The geese had decided to leave the island at dawn, but first they wanted to feed. As they walked around, nibbling, a mountain duck came up to Dunfin. "I have a message from your sisters," said the duck. "They don't dare go near Akka's flock, but they asked me to remind you not to leave the island without calling on the old fisherman."

"Oh, I would like to see him," Dunfin said, but she was so frightened now that she would not go alone. She asked the goosey-gander and Thumbietot to accompany her to the hut.

The door was open, so Dunfin entered, but the others remained outside. When they heard Akka give the signal to start, they called to Dunfin. A gray goose came out and flew with the wild geese away from the island.

They had traveled quite a distance along the archipelago when the boy began to wonder about the goose accompanying them. Dunfin always flew lightly and noiselessly, but this one labored with heavy and noisy wing strokes. "That's not Dunfin—it's Prettywing!"

The boy had barely spoken when the goose uttered such an ugly, angry shriek that everyone knew who she was. Akka and the others turned to her, but the gray goose did not fly away at once. Instead she bumped against the big goosey-gander, snatched Thumbietot and flew off with him in her bill.

There was a wild chase over the archipelago. Prettywing flew fast, but the wild geese were close behind her, and there was no chance for her to escape. Suddenly they saw a puff of smoke rise up from the sea and heard an explosion. In their excitement they hadn't realized that they were directly above a boat in which a lone fisherman was seated. Just there, above the boat, Prettywing opened her bill and dropped Thumbietot into the sea.

THE TRAVELS OF
BOOK TWO
NILS HOLGERSSON

Chapter Seven

Stockholm

Skansen

A few years ago, an old man named Clement Larsson lived at Skansen—the great park outside of Stockholm where people have collected many wonderful things. Clement was from Hälsingland and had come to Skansen with his fiddle to play folk dances and other old melodies. As a performer, he appeared mostly in the evening. During the day it was his business to sit on guard in one of the many pretty peasant cottages which have been moved to Skansen from all parts of the country.

At first Clement thought that he was better off in his old age than he had ever dared dream, but as time went by, he began to dislike the place, especially when he was on guard duty. It was all right when visitors came into the cottage to look around, but some days Clement would sit for hours all alone. Then he felt so homesick that he feared he would have to leave. He was poor and knew that at home he would become a charge of the parish, so he tried to hold out as long as he could.

One beautiful evening in the beginning of May, Clement had been granted a few hours' leave of absence. He was on his way down the steep hill leading out of Skansen, when he met an island fisherman coming along with his game bag. The fisherman was a young man who often came to Skansen with sea birds that he had managed to capture alive. Clement had talked to him many times.

The fisherman stopped Clement to ask if the superintendent at Skansen was at home. Clement told him and then asked what he had in his bag.

"I'll show you," said the fisherman, "if you'll give me an idea what price I should ask for it."

He opened the bag, and Clement looked into it—once, and again, and then drew back a step or two. "Good gracious, Asbjörn! How did you catch that?" he exclaimed.

Clement remembered that when he was a child, his mother used to talk of the tiny folk who lived under the cabin floor. He wasn't allowed to cry or to be naughty; otherwise he might provoke the little people. Later as an adult, he believed his mother had made up the stories about the tomten to make him behave himself. Now he thought differently. It had been no invention of his mother's; why there, in Asbjörn's bag, lay one of the tiny folk.

Clement felt some of the terror natural to childhood. Asbjörn saw that he was frightened and began to laugh, but Clement took the matter seriously.

"Tell me, Asbjörn. Where did you find him?"

"You may be sure I wasn't looking for him," said Asbjörn. "He came to me. I started out early this morning and took my rifle along into the boat. I'd just poled away from shore when I saw wild geese coming from the east. They were shrieking like mad. I shot at them, but didn't hit any. Instead this creature fell into the water—so close to the boat that I only had to put my hand out and pick him up."

"I hope you didn't shoot him, Asbjörn."

"Oh, no! He's well enough. When he came down, though, he was dazed. I took advantage of that to wind the ends of two sail threads around his ankles and wrists so he couldn't run away. 'Ha! Here's something for Skansen,' I thought."

Clement grew more troubled as the fisherman talked. All that he had heard about the tiny folk in his childhood—of their vindictiveness toward enemies and kindness toward friends—came back to him. It had never gone well with those who had attempted to hold one of them captive.

"You should have let him go at once, Asbjörn," said Clement.

"I was nearly forced to set him free," replied the fisherman. "The wild geese followed me all the way home, and they criss-crossed over the island all morning, honking as if they wanted him back. Not only they, but the entire population—sea gulls, sea swallows, and many others that aren't worth a shot of pow-der—landed on the island and made an awful racket.

When I came out, they fluttered around me until I had to turn back. My wife begged me to let him go, but I'd made up my mind to take him to Skansen. I put one of the children's dolls in the window, hid the little fellow in the bottom of my bag, and left. The birds must've thought it was he who stood in the win-dow, because they let me leave without pursuing me."

"Does he say anything?" asked Clement.

"Yes. He tried to call to the birds, but I gagged him."

"Oh, Asbjörn!" protested Clement. "How could you treat him like that? Don't you realize he is supernatural?"

"I don't know what he is," said Asbjörn. "Let others consid-er that possibility. I'll be satisfied if I can sell him for a good sum of money. How much do you think the doctor at Skansen would give me for him?"

There was a long pause before Clement replied. He felt sorry for the poor little creature. He actually imagined that his mother was standing beside him telling him to be kind to the tiny folk.

"I have no idea what the doctor up there would care to give you, Asbjörn," he said, "but if you leave him with me, I'll give you twenty kroner."

Asbjörn stared at the fiddler. Twenty kroner! He thought Clement must believe the tomten had some mysterious power that could be put to use. He was by no means certain that the doctor would think the creature was such a great find or would offer to pay so high a sum for him, so he accepted Clement's offer.

The fiddler poked his purchase into one of his wide pockets, turned back to Skansen and entered a moss-covered hut where there were neither visitors nor guards. He closed the door after him, took out the tiny one, who was still bound hand and foot and gagged, and gently laid him on a bench.

"Listen," said Clement. "I know that you don't like to be seen by people. I've decided to set you free, but only on the condition that you will remain in this park until I allow you to leave.

If you promise to abide by this condition, nod your head three times."

Clement gazed at the tomten, fully expecting him to do as he was told, but the tomten did not move a muscle.

"I'll see to it that you are fed every day, and you will have so much to do there that the time won't seem long to you. It's just that you cannot leave until I give you permission. When I set your food out in a white bowl, that means you are to stay. When I set it out in a blue one, you may go."

Clement waited for a response, but again the tomten did not stir.

"Very well," said Clement, "then there's nothing to do but show you to the master of this place. Then you'll be put into a glass case, and all the people in the big city of Stockholm will come and stare at you."

This scared the tomten, and he promptly gave the signal Clement wanted; he nodded three times.

"Good," said Clement, and he cut the cord that bound the tomten's hands. Then he hurried toward the door.

The boy untied the bands around his ankles and tore away the gag, but when he turned to Clement to thank him, the old man had gone.

........................◆........................

Just outside the door Clement met a handsome, noble-looking gentleman, who was on his way to a place close by from which there was a scenic view. Clement could not recall having seen the stately old man before, but the latter must have seen Clement playing the fiddle at one time or another because he stopped and spoke to him.

"Good day, Clement," he said. "Are you ill? You seem to have grown a bit thin."

There was such an expression of kindliness about the old gentleman that Clement felt free to mention his homesickness.

"What?" said the old gentleman. "Are you homesick in Stockholm? That's impossible!" He seemed offended. Then the gentleman reflected that the person he was talking to mustn't know much about the city.

"Haven't you heard how the city of Stockholm was founded? If you had, you would know that your desire to leave is absurd.

"Come with me." He led Clement over to a bench positioned at the scenic overlook. When the old gentlemen was seated, he glanced down at the city, which spread in all its glory below him, and he drew a deep breath as if he wished to drink in all the beauty of the landscape. Then he turned to the fiddler.

"Look, Clement," he said. As he talked, he traced with his cane a little map in the sand in front of them. "Here lies Uppland. Here, to the south, a point juts out; it's split up by bays. Here we have Sörmland with another point, which is just as cut up and points straight north. Here, from the west, is a lake filled with islands—Mälaren. From the east comes another body of water, which can barely squeeze in among the islands and islets. It is the East Sea. Here, Clement, where Uppland joins Sörmland and Mälaren joins the East Sea, comes a short river, in the center of which lie four little islands that divide the river into tributaries—one of which is called Norriström but was formerly Stocksund.

"In the beginning these little islands were ordinary wooded islands, like the ones on Mälaren even today, and for ages they were entirely uninhabited. They were well located between two bodies of water and two bodies of land. Year after year passed. People settled along Mälaren and in the archipelago, but these

river islands didn't attract any settlers at all. On occasion, of course, a seafarer happened to port at one of them and pitched his tent for the night, but no one remained there long.

"One day a fisherman, who lived on Liding Island out in Salt Fjord, steered his boat toward Lake Mälar. He had such good luck with his fishing that he forgot to start for home in time. He got no farther than the four little islands, and the best he could do was to land on one and wait till later in the night for bright moonlight.

"It was late summer and warm. The fisherman hauled his boat on land, lay down beside it, his head resting upon a stone, and fell asleep. When he awoke, the moon had been up a long while. It hung right above him and shone like broad daylight.

"The man jumped to his feet and was about to push his boat into the water, when he saw some black specks moving out in the stream, apparently headed toward shore. He bent down for his spear, which he always kept with him in the boat.

"When he straightened up, however, he didn't see seals. Beautiful young maidens stood on the strand. They were dressed in green, trailing satin robes, with pearl crowns on their heads.

"They were mermaids. They lived on desolate rock islands far out at sea, and these had worn seal disguises so they could come up on land and enjoy the moonlight on the green islands.

"He laid down the spear very cautiously. When the girls came up on the island to play, he stole up from behind and watched them. He'd heard that sea nymphs were so beautiful and fascinating that no one could see them and not be enchanted by their charms. Now he believed what he had heard.

"After he had stood for awhile under the shadow of the trees and watched the mermaids dance, he went down to the strand. He stole one of the seal skins lying there and hid it under a stone. Then he went back to his boat, lay down beside it and pretended to be asleep.

"Before long he saw the girls trip down to the strand to dress in their seal skins. At first all was play and laughter...which changed to frightened crying when one of the mermaids couldn't find her seal robe. She and her companions ran up and down the

strand, searching for it, but they couldn't find a trace of it.

"The sky was growing pale and day was breaking, so the mermaids had to leave. They swam away, leaving behind the one whose seal skin was missing. She sat on the strand and wept.

"The fisherman felt sorry for her, but he lay still until daybreak. Then he got up, pushed the boat into the water, and stepped into it to make it seem as though he noticed her by chance after he had lifted the oars.

"'Who are you?' he called out. 'Have you been shipwrecked?'

"She ran toward him and asked if he had seen her seal skin. The fisherman pretended not to know what she was talking about. She sat down again and wept.

"He decided to take her with him in the boat. 'Come with me to my cottage,' he said. 'My mother will take care of you. You can't stay here on the island, without food and shelter.'

"He talked so convincingly that she was persuaded to get into his boat. Both the fisherman and his mother were kind to the poor mermaid, and she seemed to be happy with them. She grew more contented every day and helped the older woman with her work, and was exactly like any other island lass...only she was much prettier.

"One day the fisherman asked her if she would be his wife, and she didn't object. Wedding preparations were made. The mermaid dressed as a bride in her green, trailing robe with the shimmering pearl crown she had worn when the fisherman first saw her.

"There was no church nor parson on the island then, so the bridal party seated themselves in boats to row up to the first church they saw. The fisherman had the mermaid and his mother in his boat, and he rowed so well that he was far ahead of the others. When he had gotten far enough to see the island in the river where he won his bride, he could not help smiling.

"'What are you smiling about?' she asked.

"'Oh, I'm thinking of the night when I hid your seal skin,' answered the fisherman, for he thought there was no longer any need for him to conceal anything.

"'What?' said his startled bride. 'I have never owned a seal skin.'

"'Don't you remember how you danced with the mermaids?' he asked her.

"'I don't know what you mean,' said the bride. 'You must have had a strange dream last night.'

"'If I show you your seal skin, you will probably believe me,' laughed the fisherman, promptly turning the boat toward the little island. They stepped ashore, and he pulled the seal skin out from under the stone where he had hidden it.

"The instant the bride saw her seal skin, she seized it and drew it over her head. It snuggled close to her—as though there were life in it—and she dove into the stream.

"The bridegroom saw her swim away and plunged into the water after her. He couldn't catch her. When he saw that he couldn't stop her any other way, he hurled his spear at her. He aimed even better than he had intended, because the mermaid gave a piercing cry and disappeared in the depths.

"The fisherman stood on the strand waiting for her to appear again. The water around him began to take on a soft sheen, a beauty that he had never seen before. It shimmered in pink and white, like the color play on the inside of sea shells.

"As the glittering water lapped the shores, the fisherman thought that they, too, had been transformed. They began to blossom and waft their perfumes. A soft sheen spread over them, and they took on a beauty they had never possessed before.

"So it is with mermaids: even what the mermaids have touched takes on their beauty. So when the mermaid's blood mixed with the water that bathed the shores, her beauty was transferred to both. All who saw them must love and yearn for them. This was their legacy from the mermaid."

When the stately old gentleman had gotten this far in his narrative, he turned to Clement and looked at him. Clement nodded politely but made no comment; he did not want to cause a break in the story.

"Bear this in mind, Clement," the old gentleman continued, with a teasing gleam in his eyes. "From that time on, people moved to these islands. At first only fishermen and peasants settled there, but others, too, were attracted to them. One day the king and his earl sailed up the stream. They started to talk about these islands, having seen that they were located so every vessel that sailed toward Lake Mälar had to pass them. The earl suggested that a lock be put on the channel—one that could be opened or closed at will—to let in merchant vessels and shut out pirates.

"This idea was carried out," said the old gentleman. He stood up and began to trace in the sand again with his cane. "On the largest of these islands the earl erected a fortress with a strong tower, which was called Kärnan. Then a wall was built around the island. Here, at the north and south ends of the wall, craftsmen made gates and erected strong towers over them. Across the other islands they built bridges, and these were also equipped with high towers. Out in the water, round about, they put a wreath of piles with bars that could open and close, so that no vessel could sail past without permission.

"You see, Clement, the four islands that had lain unnoticed for so long were soon strongly fortified. The shores and the sound attracted more people, and they came from all around to settle there. They built a church, which has since been called Storkyrkan. Here it stands, near the castle. And here, within the walls, the peasants built little huts. They were primitive, but they served their purpose; they were enough to make the place a city, and the city was named Stockholm.

"One day, Clement, the earl who had begun the work went to his final rest, and Stockholm was without a master builder. Monks called the Gray Friars came to the country, and Stockholm attracted them. They asked permission to erect a monastery there, and the king gave them an island—one of the smaller ones...this one facing Lake Mälar. Here they built, and the place was called Gray Friars' Island.

"Other monks came, called the Black Friars. They, too, asked for the right to build in Stockholm, near the south gate. On this, the larger of the islands north of the city, a Holy Ghost House—a hospital—was built. On the smaller of the islands, thrifty men put up a mill, and along the little islands close by, the monks fished. As you know, there is only one island now, for the canal between the two has filled up; that island is still called Holy Ghost Island.

"All of the little wooded islands were dotted with houses. Still people streamed in because these shores and waters have the

power to draw them. Pious women of the Order of Saint Clara came and asked for ground to build upon. They had no choice but to settle on the north shore—at Norrmalm, as it is called. They weren't pleased with the location because across Norrmalm ran a high ridge, where the city had its gallows hill; it was a detested spot. The Poor Clares erected their church and their convent on the strand below the ridge. As soon as they were established there, they found plenty of followers in spite of the location. Upon the ridge itself they built a hospital and a church dedicated to Saint Göran. Just below the ridge a church was erected to Saint Jacob. Even at Södermalm, where the mountain rises straight up from the strand, they began to build. There they raised a church in honor of Saint Mary.

"Not only cloister folk moved to Stockholm, of course. Others did, too—principally German tradesmen and artisans. They were more skilled than the Swedes and were welcomed. They settled within the walls of the city. They pulled down the wretched little cabins and built high, magnificent stone houses. Since there wasn't much space within the walls, however, they had to build the houses close together, with gables facing narrow lanes.

"So you see, Clement, Stockholm attracted people."

At this point in the narrative another gentleman appeared, walking quickly down the path toward the man who was speaking to Clement. The seated gentleman waved to him, and he remained at a distance.

"Now, Clement, you must do something for me," he said. "I don't have more time to talk with you, but I will send you a book about Stockholm. Read it from cover to cover.

"I have, so to speak, laid the foundations of Stockholm for you. Read about it for yourself. You will learn how the city has thrived and changed. Read how the little, narrow, wall-enclosed city on the islands has spread into this great sea of houses below us. Read how, on the spot where the dark tower Kärnan once stood, the beautiful, light castle below us was erected and how the Gray Friars' church was turned into the burial place of the Swedish kings. Discover for yourself how island after island was built up with factories, how the ridge was lowered and the sound filled in, how the truck gardens at the south and north ends of the city were converted into beautiful parks and built-up quarters, how the king's private deer park became the people's favorite pleasure resort. Make yourself at home here, Clement. This city belongs not only to Stockholmers, but to you and to all Swedes.

"As you read about Stockholm, remember that I have spoken the truth; this city has the power to draw everyone to it. First the king moved here. Then the nobles built their palaces here. One after another was attracted to the place, so that now, as you see, Stockholm is not a city unto itself or for nearby districts; it has grown into a city for the whole kingdom.

"You know, Clement, that there are judicial courts in every parish throughout the land, but in Stockholm they have jurisdiction over the whole nation. You know that there are judges in every district court in the country, but at Stockholm there is only one court, to which all the others are accountable. You know there are barracks and troops in every part of the land, but those in Stockholm command the whole army. Everywhere in the country you will find railroads, but the whole great national system is controlled and managed in Stockholm. Here you will find the governing boards for the clergy, for teachers, for physicians, for bailiffs and jurors.

"This is the heart of your country, Clement. All the change you have in your pocket is coined here, and the postage stamps you stick on your letters are made here. There is something here for every Swede. Here no one need feel homesick, for here all Swedes are at home.

"When you read of all that has been brought here to Stockholm, think too of the latest that the city has attracted: these old-fashioned peasant cottages at Skansen, the old dances, the old costumes and house furnishings, the musicians and storytellers. Stockholm has drawn all the good things of the old days here to Skansen.

"First and last, see how the waves around Stockholm sparkle in joyous play...how the shores shimmer with beauty.

You will come under their spell, Clement."

The handsome old gentleman had raised his voice, so that it rang out strong and commanding. Then he stood up. With a wave of his hand to Clement, he walked away. Clement realized that he was a great man, and he bowed to him as low as he could.

........................◆........................

The next day, a royal lackey (liveried servant) brought a big red book and a letter for Clement; the book was from the king. After that, the little old man, Clement Larsson, was lightheaded for several days, and it was impossible to get a sensible word out of him. After a week had gone by, he went to the superintendent and resigned from his position. He had to go home.

"Why must you go home? Can't you learn to be content here?" asked the doctor.

"Oh, I am," said Clement. "That matter no longer troubles me. I have to go home anyway."

It did bother Clement that the king had said that he should learn all about Stockholm and be happy there, but in spite of that, he couldn't rest until he had told everyone at home what had happened. He couldn't possibly drop the idea of standing on the church knoll at home and telling high and low that the king had been so kind to him, that he had sat beside him on the bench, and had sent him a book, and had taken the time to talk to him—a poor fiddler—for a whole hour, in order to cure him of his homesickness. It was fine to relate this to the Laplanders and Dalecarlian peasant girls at Skansen, but what was that compared to being able to tell of it at home?

Even if Clement were to end in the poorhouse, it wouldn't be so hard after this. He was a totally different man from what he had been, and he would be respected and honored in a very different way.

Chapter Eight

Gorgo, the Eagle

In the Mountain Glen
....

F ar up the mountains of Lapland there was an old eagles' nest on a ledge that projected from a high cliff. The nest was made of dry twigs of pine and spruce, interlaced until they formed a perfect network. Year after year the nest had been repaired and strengthened. It was about two yards wide and nearly as high as a Laplander's hut.

The cliff where the eagles' nest rested towered above a big glen, which was inhabited in summer by a flock of wild geese. The glen was an excellent refuge for them; it was so secluded that not many knew of it, even among the Laplanders themselves. In the heart of this glen there was a small, round lake containing an abundance of food for the tiny goslings. On the lakeshores, which were covered with osier bushes and small birches, the geese found nesting places.

Eagles had always lived on the mountain, and geese in the glen. Every year the eagles carried off a few of the geese, but were careful not to take so many that the wild geese would be afraid to remain in the glen. The geese, in their turn, found the eagles quite useful. They were robbers, to be sure, but they kept other robbers away.

Two years before Nils Holgersson traveled with the wild geese, the old leader goose, Akka from Kebnekaise, was standing at the foot of the mountain slope. She was looking at the eagles' nest.

The eagles were in the habit of starting on their chase soon after sunrise. In the summers that Akka had lived in the glen, she had watched every morning for the eagles' departure to see if they stopped in the glen to hunt or if they flew beyond it to other hunting grounds.

She did not have to wait long before the two eagles left the ledge on the cliff. Stately and terrifying, they soared into the air. They directed their course toward the plain, and Akka breathed a sigh of relief.

The old leader goose's days of nesting and rearing young were over, and during the summer she passed the time going from one goose range to another, giving counsel about the care of the young. Aside from this she kept an eye out not only for eagles but also for mountain fox, owls and all other enemies who were a menace to the wild geese and their young.

About noon, Akka began to watch for the eagles again. This she had done every day during the summers she had lived in the glen. She could tell at once by their flight if their hunt had been successful, and in that event she felt sure of the safety of those who belonged to her. On this particular day, though, she had not seen the eagles return.

"I must be getting old and senile," she thought, after she had waited some time for them. "The eagles have probably been home all this time."

In the afternoon she looked toward the cliff again, expecting to see the eagles perched on the rocky ledge where they usually took their afternoon rest. Toward evening, when they took their bath in the dale lake, she tried again to catch sight of them, but failed. Again she moaned over the fact that she was growing old. She was so accustomed to having the eagles on the mountain above her that she could not imagine the possibility of their not having returned. She would have to awaken earlier.

The following morning Akka was awake in plenty of time to watch for the eagles, but again she did not see them. In the morning stillness, she heard a cry that sounded both angry and plaintive, and it seemed to come from the eagles' nest.

"Could something have happened to the eagles?" she wondered.

She spread her wings and rose high enough to look down into the nest. Neither of the adult eagles were there, but only a little, half-fledged eaglet screaming for food.

Akka sank down toward the eagles' nest, slowly and reluctantly. It was a gruesome place. It was obvious what kind of robbers lived there. In the nest and on the cliff ledge lay bleached bones, bloody feathers, pieces of skin, hares' heads, birds' beaks, and the tufted claws of grouse. The eaglet, who was lying in the midst of this, was repulsive, with his big, gaping beak, his awkward, down-covered body, and his undeveloped wings where the prospective quills stuck out like thorns.

Akka conquered her repugnance and alighted on the edge of the nest, at the same time glancing about her anxiously in every direction, expecting to see the parent eagles coming back at any moment.

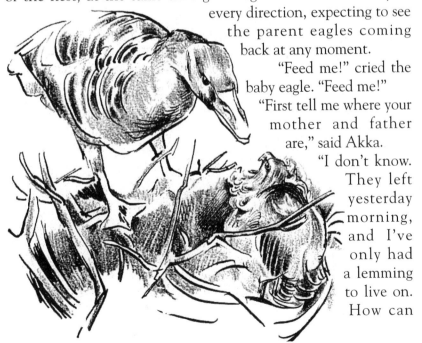

"Feed me!" cried the baby eagle. "Feed me!"

"First tell me where your mother and father are," said Akka.

"I don't know. They left yesterday morning, and I've only had a lemming to live on. How can

Mother starve me like this? *You* feed me! Feed me! Feed me!"

Akka began to think that the eagles had really been shot. If she were to let the eaglet starve she might perhaps be rid of the whole robber tribe, but it went against her to neglect a deserted young one.

"Why do you just sit there and stare?" snapped the eaglet. "Didn't you hear me say I wanted food?"

Akka spread her wings and sank down to the little lake in the glen. A moment later she returned to the eagles' nest with a salmon in her bill.

The eaglet flew into a tantrum when she dropped the fish in front of him. "Do you expect me to eat that? Ick!" he shrieked, pushing it away and trying to strike Akka with his bill. "Get me a willow grouse or a lemming, do you hear?"

Akka stretched her head forward and gave him a sharp nip in the neck. "If I'm to get food for you, you must be satisfied with what I give you. Your father and mother are dead; they can't help you. If you want to lie here and starve while you wait for grouse and lemming, I won't stop you."

After Akka had spoken her mind, she promptly left and did not return for some time. When she did return, the eaglet had eaten the fish, and when she dropped another one in front of him, he swallowed it even if he didn't like it.

Akka had imposed upon herself a tedious task. The old eagles never appeared again, and she alone had to get the eaglet all the food he needed. She gave him fish and frogs, and he seemed to do well on this diet. He grew big and strong. He soon forgot his parents, the eagles, and thought Akka was his real mother. Akka, in turn, loved him as if he had been her own child. She tried to give him a good bringing up, and to cure him of his wildness and overbearing ways.

After a couple of weeks, Akka realized that the time was coming for her to molt and put on a new feather dress so as to be ready to fly. For a whole moon she would be unable to carry food to the baby eaglet, and this time he might starve.

One day Akka said to him: "Gorgo, I can no longer bring fish up to your nest. Everything depends upon your courage. Do you dare to venture into the glen so I can continue to get food for you? You must choose between starvation and flying down to the glen. Even flying, since you have never done it before, may cost you your life."

Without hesitating, the eaglet stepped upon the edge of the nest. Barely taking the trouble to measure the distance to the bottom, he spread his tiny wings and started away. He rolled over and over in space, but made enough use of his wings to reach the ground almost unhurt.

Down there in the glen Gorgo passed the summer in company with the little goslings and was a good friend to them. Since he thought he too was a gosling, he tried to do the things they did. When they swam in the lake, he followed them until he nearly drowned. He was embarrassed by that, and he asked Akka, "Why can't I swim like the others?"

"Your claws grew too hooked and your toes too large while you were up on the cliff," Akka replied, "but you will make a fine bird anyway."

The eaglet's wings soon grew large enough to carry him, but it wasn't until autumn, when the goslings learned to fly, that it dawned on him that he could use his wings for flight. In practically no time at all, at this sport he was the best of them all. His companions never stayed up in the air any longer than they had to, but he stayed there most of the day, practicing the art of flying.

It still hadn't occurred to him that he was of another bird species, but he could not help but see differences, and he questioned Akka constantly. "Why do grouse and lemming run and hide when they see my shadow on the cliff?" he asked. "They aren't afraid of the other goslings."

"Your wings grew too big when you were on the cliff," said Akka. "It's their size that frightens the little animals. Don't be unhappy because of that. You will be a fine bird all the same."

After the eagle had learned to fly, he taught himself to fish and to catch frogs. In time, he began to question this also. "Why do I live on fish and frogs?" he asked. "The other goslings don't."

"It's because I had no other food to give you when you were

on the cliff," said Akka. "Don't let that make you sad. You will be a fine bird."

When the wild geese began their autumn moving, Gorgo flew along with the flock, regarding himself all the while as one of them. The air was filled with birds who were on their way south, and there was great excitement among them when Akka appeared with an eagle in her train. The flock was continually surrounded by swarms of curious birds who loudly expressed their astonishment. Akka told them to be quiet, but it was impossible to stop the wagging tongues.

"Why do they call me an eagle?" Gorgo asked repeatedly, growing more and more exasperated. "Can't they see that I'm a wild goose? I'm no bird eater who preys upon his kind. How dare they give me such an ugly name?"

One day they flew above a barnyard where chickens were pecking on a garbage heap. "An eagle! An eagle!" clucked the chickens in a frenzy, and they started to run for shelter. Gorgo, who had heard the eagles spoken of as savage criminals, could not control his anger this time. He snapped his wings together and shot down to the ground, striking his talons into a hen. "I'll teach you that I'm no eagle!" he screamed furiously, and struck with his beak.

That instant he heard Akka call to him from the air, and he rose obediently. The wild goose flew at him. "What were you doing?" she demanded, beating him with her bill. "Were you going to tear that hen to pieces?"

When the eagle took his punishment from the wild goose without a protest, there arose a storm of taunts from the bird throng around them. Gorgo turned toward Akka with flaming eyes, as though he would have liked to attack her. Suddenly he flew high into the sky, where no call could reach him.

Two days later he returned. "I know who I am," he said to Akka. "I must be true to my heritage, but let's be friends anyway. I promise never to attack you and your friends."

Akka was disappointed. She had set her heart on successfully training the eagle to be a mild and harmless bird, and could not tolerate his wanting to do as he chose. "Do you think I want to be the friend of a bird eater?" she asked. "Live as I have taught you to live. Only then may you travel with my flock."

Both birds were proud and stubborn, and neither would yield. It ended in Akka's forbidding the eagle to show his face in her neighborhood, and her anger toward him was so intense that no one dared mention his name in her presence.

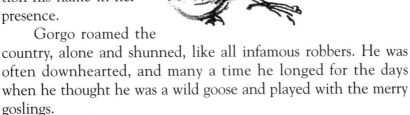

Gorgo roamed the country, alone and shunned, like all infamous robbers. He was often downhearted, and many a time he longed for the days when he thought he was a wild goose and played with the merry goslings.

Among the animals, however, he gained a reputation for great courage. They used to say that he feared no one but his foster mother, Akka. They could also say of him that he never used violence against a wild goose.

In Captivity

Gorgo was only three years old and had not yet thought about marrying and procuring a home for himself when, one day, he was captured by a hunter and sold to the Skansen Zoological Garden. Two eagles were already held captive in a cage built of iron bars and steel wires. The cage stood out in the open and was so large that two trees had been moved into it and a large cairn (heap of stones) was piled in there.

The two captive birds sat motionless all day long. Their pretty, dark feather dresses were rough and lusterless, and their eyes were riveted with hopeless longing on the sky above.

During the first week of Gorgo's captivity he was still awake and full of life, but a heavy torpor gradually came upon him. He perched on one spot, like the other eagles, and stared vacantly. He no longer paid attention to the passing days.

One morning he heard someone call to him from below. He could barely rouse himself enough to look down. "Who's calling me?" he asked.

"Gorgo! Don't you know me? I'm Thumbietot, who used to fly with the wild geese."

"Has Akka been captured?" asked Gorgo in the tone of one who is trying to collect his thoughts after a long sleep.

"No, no. Akka, the white goosey-gander and the whole flock are probably safe and sound up in Lapland by now," said the boy.

Gorgo looked away again.

"Golden eagle!" shouted the boy, "I have not forgotten the time you carried me back to the wild geese and that you spared the white goosey-gander's life. Can I be of help to you?"

"Don't disturb me, Thumbietot," Gorgo yawned. "I'm dreaming that I am free and soaring away up among the clouds. I don't want to be awake."

"Shake yourself and see what is going on around you," the boy admonished, "or you will soon look as wretched as the other eagles."

"I wish I were like them," Gorgo replied. "They're so lost in their dreams that nothing can trouble them."

When night came and all three eagles were asleep, there was a light scraping on the steel wires stretched across the top of the cage. The two listless old captives did not allow themselves to be disturbed by the noise, but Gorgo awakened. "Who's there?" he asked.

"It's Thumbietot, Gorgo," answered the boy. "I'm filing the steel wires so you can escape."

The eagle raised his head and saw in the night light that the boy was sitting on top of his cage, filing wires. For a moment he felt hopeful, but then he said, "I'm a big bird, Thumbietot. How could you ever file away enough wires for me to get out? Quit and leave me in peace."

"Go to sleep, and don't bother about me," said the boy. "I won't be done tonight or even tomorrow night, but I will try to free you before you become a total wreck in this place."

Gorgo fell asleep. When he woke the next morning, he saw at a glance that a number of wires had been filed. That day he felt less drowsy. He spread his wings and fluttered from branch to branch to get the stiffness out of his joints.

Early one morning, just as the first streak of sunlight made its appearance, Thumbietot awakened the eagle. "Try to get out, Gorgo," he whispered.

The eagle looked up. The boy had filed off so many wires that there was a big hole in the netting. Gorgo flapped his wings and propelled himself upward. Twice he missed and fell back into the cage, but finally he succeeded.

With proud wing strokes he soared into the clouds. Little Thumbietot sat and gazed after him with a mournful expression. He wished that someone would give him his freedom too.

The boy now lived at Skansen. He had become acquainted with all of the animals there and made many friends. He had to admit that there was so much to see and learn that it was not difficult for him to pass the time. Of course his thoughts turned to Morton Goosey-Gander and his other comrades, and he wished he were with them. "If only I weren't bound to my promise to Clement, I'd find a bird to take me to my friends."

It may seem strange that Clement Larsson had not restored the boy's liberty, but one must remember how excited the fiddler had been when he left Skansen. The morning of his departure he had thought of setting out the tomten's food in a blue bowl, but, unfortunately, he'd been unable to find one. All the Skansen folk—Lapps, peasant girls, artisans and gardeners—had come to tell him good-bye, and he had had no time to search for a blue bowl. It was time to start, and at the last minute he had to ask an old Laplander to help him.

"One of the tiny folk happens to be living here at Skansen," said Clement, "and every morning I set out food for him. Will you do me the favor of taking these few coppers and purchasing a blue bowl with them? Put a little gruel and milk in it, and tomorrow morning set it out under the steps of the Bollnäs cottage."

The old Laplander looked surprised, but there was no time for Clement to explain further; he had to leave for the train station. The Laplander went down to the zoological village to purchase the bowl. He didn't see a blue one that he felt appropriate, so he bought a white one, and this he conscientiously filled and set out every morning. That was why the boy had not been released from his pledge.

Nils knew that Clement had gone away, but why wasn't he allowed to go? That night the boy longed more than ever for his freedom...and especially now in the summertime. During the winter he had suffered in the cold and stormy weather, and when he first came to Skansen he had thought that perhaps it was just as well that he had been forced to break the journey. He would have frozen to death if he had gone to Lapland in the month of May, but now it was warm. The earth was clad in green, birches and poplars were clothed in satiny foliage, and the cherry trees— in fact, all the fruit trees—were covered with blossoms. The berry bushes had green berries on their stems. The oaks had carefully unfolded their leaves, and peas, cabbages and beans were growing in the vegetable garden in Skansen.

"Lapland must be warm by this time," thought the boy. "Oh, how I would like to be seated on Morton Goosey-Gander's back on a fine morning like this. It would be fun to ride around in the warm, still air, looking down at the ground now that it's all decked out with green grass and pretty blossoms."

He sat musing on this when the eagle suddenly swooped down from the sky and perched beside him, on top of the cage.

"I tried my wings to see if they were still good for anything," said Gorgo. "You didn't suppose I meant to leave you here in captivity, did you? Get up on my back, and I'll take you to your friends."

"That's impossible," the boy answered. "I have pledged my word that I would stay here until I am liberated."

"What sort of nonsense is that?" protested Gorgo. "In the first place you were brought here against your will. Then you were forced to promise that you would stay here. That's not a promise worth keeping."

"Oh, but I must keep it," said the boy. "Thank you all the same for your kind intention, but you can't help me."

"Can't I, though?" said Gorgo. "We'll see about that." In a twinkling he grasped Nils Holgersson in his big talons and rose with him toward the sky, disappearing in a northerly direction.

On Over Gästrikland

The Precious Belt
....

The eagle kept on flying until he was far north of Stockholm. Then he sank to a wooded hill, where he relaxed his hold on the boy. Thumbietot started to run back to the city as fast as he could. The eagle made a swoop and stopped him.

"Do you want to go back to prison?" he demanded.

"That's my business. I can go where I like, no matter what you think!" retorted the boy, trying to get away.

The eagle gripped him with his strong talons and rose into the sky. He circled over the entire province of Uppland and did not stop again until he got to the waterfalls at Älvkarleby, where he alighted on a rock in the middle of the rushing rapids below the roaring falls. Again he relaxed his hold on the captive.

The boy saw no way to escape. Above them the white scum wall of the waterfall tumbled down, and the river rushed along in a mighty torrent. To think that he had been forced to become a promise breaker! Thumbietot was indignant; he turned his back to the eagle and wouldn't speak to him.

Now that the bird had set the boy down in a place from which he could not run away, he told him that he had been brought up by Akka from Kebnekaise and that he had quarreled with his foster mother.

"Maybe now you understand why I want to take you back to the wild geese, Thumbietot. I have heard that Akka esteems you highly, and it's been my intention to ask you to make peace between us."

As soon as the boy understood that the eagle had not carried him off out of sheer spite, he said, "I would like to help you," he said, "but I'm bound by my promise." He explained to the eagle how he had fallen into captivity and how Clement Larsson had left Skansen without setting him free.

In spite of his patient explanation, the eagle would not give up his plan. "Listen, Thumbietot," he said. "My wings can carry you wherever you want to go, and my eyes can search out whatever you want to find. Tell me what Clement Larsson looks like; I will find him and take you to him."

Thumbietot quickly agreed. "I can see that you have had a wise bird like Akka for a foster mother," he said. Then he described Clement, adding that he had heard at Skansen that the little fiddler was from Hälsingland.

"We'll look for him through the whole of Hälsingland—from Ljungby to Mellansjö, from Great Mountain to Hornland," said the eagle. "Tomorrow before sundown you shall have a talk with the man."

"I fear you are promising more than you can perform," doubted the boy.

"I would be a sorry excuse for an eagle if I couldn't do that much," said Gorgo.

So when Gorgo and Thumbietot left Älvkarleby, they were good friends. The boy willingly took a ride on the eagle's back, and thus he had an opportunity to see much of the country.

While clutched in the eagle's talons, he hadn't seen anything. Perhaps it was just as well, for in the morning he had traveled over Uppsala, Österby's big factories, the Dannemora Mine and the ancient castle of Örbyhus, and he would have been sadly

disappointed at not seeing them had he known how close they were. The eagle raced over Gästrikland. In the southern part of the province there was little to see, but the trip grew more interesting as they flew north.

"The country is dressed in a spruce skirt and a graystone jacket," thought the boy, "and around its waist is a belt so wonderful, it's beyond comparison. It's embroidered with blue lakes and green groves; the great ironworks adorn it like a row of precious stones; and its buckle is a whole city with castles, cathedrals and great clusters of houses."

When the travelers arrived in the northern forest, Gorgo alighted on top of a mountain. As the boy dismounted, the eagle said, "There's game in this forest, and I simply can't forget my captivity and feel free until I have gone hunting. You won't mind my leaving you for awhile?"

"No, of course I won't," the boy assured him.

"Go where you like, but be back here by sundown," called the eagle as he flew off.

The boy sat on a stone, gazing across the bare, rocky ground and the great forest. He felt lonely, but soon he heard singing in the forest below and saw something bright moving among the trees. Then he saw a blue and yellow banner, and he knew by the songs and the merry chatter that it was being borne at the head of a procession.

On it went, up the winding path. He wondered where it and those who followed it were going. He couldn't believe that anyone would willingly come up to such an ugly, desolate waste as this. The banner was nearing the forest border, and behind it marched happy people for whom it had led the way. Suddenly there was life and movement all over the mountain plain. After that there was so much for the boy to see that he didn't have a single dull moment.

Forest Day

On the mountain's broad back, where Gorgo left Thumbietot, there had been a forest fire. In the following ten years, the charred trees had been felled and removed, and the fire-swept area had begun to deck itself with green along the edges, where it skirted the healthy forest. The larger part of the top was still barren and appallingly desolate. Charred stumps, standing sentinel-like among the rock ledges, bore witness that once there had been a fine forest here, but no fresh roots peeked up from the ground.

On this early summer day, all the children in the parish had assembled in front of the schoolhouse near the fire-swept mountain. Each child carried either a spade or a hoe on his shoulder and a basket of food in his hand. As soon as all were assembled, they marched in a long procession toward the forest. The banner went first, with the teachers on either side of it. Then followed a couple of foresters, a wagonload of pine shrubs and spruce trees, and last of all, the children.

The procession did not stop in any of the birch groves near the settlements, but marched deep into the forest. Foxes stuck their heads out of their lairs in astonishment and wondered what kind of backwoods people these were. As the procession marched past old coal pits where charcoal kilns were fired every autumn, the crossbeaks twisted their hooked bills and asked one another what kind of coalers these might be.

Finally the procession reached the big, burned mountain plain. The rocks had been stripped of the fine twin-flower creepers that once covered them; they had been robbed of the pretty silver and reindeer mosses. Around the dark water gathered in clefts and hollows, there was no longer any wood sorrel. The patches of soil in crevices and among stones were without ferns, without star flowers, without all the green and red and light and soft and soothing things which usually clothe the forest ground.

It was as if a bright light flashed upon the mountain when the parish children covered it. Here at last was something sweet and delicate, something fresh and rosy, something young and growing.

When the children had rested and eaten their lunch, they picked up their hoes and spades and began to work. The foresters showed them what to do, and they set out shrub after shrub on every clear spot of earth they could find. As they worked, they talked knowledgeably among themselves about how the little shrubs they were planting would bind the soil so that it couldn't get away and how new soil would form under the trees. In time seeds would drop, and in a few years people would be picking strawberries and raspberries where now there were only bare rocks. The little shrubs which they were planting would gradually become tall trees. Perhaps big houses and splendid ships would be built from them.

If the children hadn't come here and planted while there was still a little soil in the clefts, all the earth would have been carried away by wind and water, and the mountain would never have been clothed in green again.

"It was a good thing we came," said the children. "We were just in time." They felt very important.

While they were working on the mountain, their parents were at home. As the day went on, they wondered how the children were getting along. Of course it was only a joke about their planting a forest, but it might be amusing to see what they were trying to do.

So, fathers and mothers were on their way to the forest. When they reached the outlying stock farms, they met some of their neighbors.

"Are you going to the fire-swept mountain?" they asked.

"That's where we're bound."

"To look at the children?"

"Yes, to see what they're up to."

"It's only play, of course."

"It's not likely that the children will plant many trees. We have brought the coffee pot along so we can have something hot to drink, since we plan to stay there all day with only a basket lunch."

The children's parents went on up the mountain. At first they thought only of how pretty it looked to see all the rosy-cheeked children scattered over the gray hills. Later, they saw how the children were working—how some were setting out shrubs, others were digging furrows and sowing seeds, and others were pulling up heather to prevent its choking the young trees. They saw that the children took the work seriously and scarcely had time to glance up.

The fathers and mothers stood and looked on for awhile. Then they too began to pull up heather...just for the fun of it. The children were the instructors, because they were already trained, and had to show their parents what to do.

So it happened that all the grownups who had come to watch the children took part in the work, and the work became more fun than before. Then other implements were needed, and a couple of long-legged boys were sent down to the village for spades and hoes. As they ran past the cabins, the stay-at-homes came out and asked, "Has there been an accident?"

"No, no! The whole parish is up on the fire-swept mountain, planting a forest."

"Well, if the whole parish is there, we can't stay home."

Party after party of peasants went crowding to the top of the burned mountain. They looked for awhile, but the temptation to join the workers was irresistible.

"It's a pleasure to sow one's own acres in the spring and to think of the grain that will spring up from the earth, but this work is even more enjoyable," they thought.

Not only slender blades would come from that sowing, but mighty trees with tall trunks and sturdy branches. It meant giving birth not merely to a summer's grain, but to many years' growths. It meant the awakening hum of insects, the song of the thrush, the play of grouse and all kinds of life on the desolate mountain. It was like raising a memorial for future generations. These people could have left a bare, treeless height as a heritage; instead they were to leave a glorious forest. Coming generations would know their forefathers had been a good and wise people, and they would remember them with honor and gratitude.

Chapter Ten

A Day in Hälsingland

A Large Green Leaf

Thursday, June sixteenth.

The following day the boy traveled over Hälsingland. It spread beneath him with new, pale-green shoots on the pine trees, new birch leaves in the groves, new green grass in the meadows, and sprouting grain in the fields. It was a mountainous country, but directly through it ran a broad valley from either side of which branched other valleys—some short and narrow, some long and broad.

"This land resembles a leaf," thought the boy. "It's as green as a leaf, and the valleys divide it like the veins of a leaf."

The branch valleys, like the main one, were filled with lakes, rivers, farms and villages. They snuggled, light and smiling, between the dark mountains until they were gradually squeezed together by the hills. There they were so narrow that they could not hold more than a little brook.

On the highland between the valleys were pine forests without a bit of flat land to grow on. Mountains were all around, and the forest covered them like a woolly hide stretched over a bony body. It was a picturesque country, and the boy saw a good deal of it because the eagle was trying to find the old fiddler, Clement Larsson, and flew from ravine to ravine looking for him.

A little later in the morning there was life and movement on every farm. The doors of the cattle sheds were thrown wide open, and the cows were turned out. They were prettily colored, small, supple and sprightly, and so sure-footed that they made the most comic leaps and bounds. After them came calves and sheep, and it was plain to be seen that they, too, were in the best of spirits.

Every moment it grew busier in the farmyards. Two young girls with knapsacks on their backs walked among the cattle. A boy with a long switch kept the sheep together, and a little dog ran in and out among the cows, barking at the ones that tried to catch him on their horns. A farmer hitched a horse to a cart loaded with tubs of butter, boxes of cheese and all kinds of things to eat. People laughed and chattered. They and the animals alike were happy—as if looking forward to a day of real enjoyment.

All were on their way to the forest. One of the girls walked in the lead and coaxed the cattle with musical calls. The animals followed in a long line. The shepherd boy and the sheepdog ran here and there, to make sure no animal turned from the right course. Last came the farmer and his hired man. They walked beside the cart to prevent its being upset, because the road they followed was a narrow, stony forest path.

It may have been the custom for all the peasants in Hälsingland to send their cattle into the forests on the same day, or perhaps it only happened that year. At any rate, the boy saw processions of happy people and cattle wander out from every valley and every farm and rush into the lonely forest, filling it with life. From the depths of the dense woods, the boy heard the shepherd maidens' songs and the tinkle of cow bells. Many of the processions had long and difficult roads to travel. The boy saw how they struggled through marshes, how they had to take roundabout ways to get past fallen trees and brush, and how, time and again, carts bumped against stones and turned over with all their contents. The people met all the obstacles with jokes and laughter.

In the afternoon they came to a cleared space where cattle sheds and a couple of rude cabins had been built. The cows mooed with delight as they tramped on the luscious green grass in the yards between cabins, and began grazing. The peasants carried water and wood and all that had been brought in the carts into the larger cabin. Smoke rose from the chimney, and then the dairymaids, the shepherd boy and the men sat on a flat rock and ate their supper.

Gorgo the eagle was certain he would find Clement Larsson among the people who were on their way to the forest. Whenever he saw a stock farm procession, he sank down and scrutinized it with his sharp eyes, but hour after hour passed without his finding the person he sought.

After much circling around, toward evening they were over a stony, desolate tract east of the main valley. There the boy saw another outlying stock farm under him. The people and the cattle had arrived. The men were splitting wood, and the dairymaids were milking the cows.

"Look there!" Gorgo said. "I think we've found him."

He sank, and, to his astonishment, the boy saw that the eagle was right. There stood Clement Larsson chopping wood.

Gorgo alighted on a pine tree in the thick woods not far from the house.

"I have fulfilled my obligation," said the eagle with a toss of his head. "Now you must try to have a word with the man. I'll perch here at the top of the thick pine and wait for you."

The Animals' New Year's Eve

The day's work was done at the forest ranches, supper was over, and the peasants sat about and talked. It was a long time since they had been in the forest on a summer night, and they seemed reluctant to go to bed and sleep. It was as light as day, and the dairymaids were busy with their needlework. Now and then they raised their heads and looked toward the forest, smiling.

"We're here again," they said.

The town and all its unrest faded from their minds, and the forest with its peaceful stillness enfolded them. When at home, they had wondered how they would ever be able to endure the loneliness of the woods. Once there, they had a wonderful time.

Many of the young men and women from neighboring

ranches had come to call on them, so quite a lot of people were seated on the grass in front of the cabins. Still, they were not finding it easy to start conversation. The men were going home the next day, so the dairymaids had given them little errands and asked them to take greetings to their friends in the village. That was practically all that had been said.

Suddenly the oldest of the dairy girls looked up from her work and said: "We needn't sit in silence tonight. We have two storytellers with us. One is Clement Larsson, sitting here next to me, and the other is Bernhard from Sunnasjö; he's standing back there looking toward Black's Ridge. I think we should ask both of them to tell us a story. To the one who tells the best story, I will give the muffler I am knitting."

This proposal won hearty applause. The two competitors offered lame excuses, naturally, but were quickly persuaded. Clement asked Bernhard to begin, and he was very cooperative. He knew little about Clement Larsson but assumed that he would tell some story about ghosts and trolls. Bernhard knew people liked to listen to that sort of thing, so he thought it best to choose a ghost story himself.

................◆................

"Some centuries ago," he began, "a dean here in Delsbo township was riding through the dense forest on a New Year's Eve. He was on horseback, dressed in a fur coat and cap. On the pommel of his saddle hung a satchel in which he kept the communion service, the prayer book and his clerical robe. He had been called on a parochial errand to a remote forest settlement, where he had talked with a sick person until late in the evening. Now he was on his way home, but he was fairly sure he couldn't get back to the rectory till after midnight.

"Since he had to sit in the saddle when he'd rather have been at home in bed, he was glad it wasn't a rough night. The weather was mild, the air still and the sky overcast. Behind the clouds hung a full, round moon, which gave some light although the moon was out of sight. If it were not for that faint light, it

would have been impossible for him to distinguish paths from fields, for that was a snowless winter and everything had the same grayish-brown color.

"The horse the dean rode was one he prized. He was strong and sturdy, and quite as smart as a human being. He could find his way home from anywhere in the township. The dean had observed this on several occasions, and he relied upon it with such a sense of security that he never worried where he was going when he rode that horse. So he went along in the gray night, through the bewildering forest, with the reins dangling and his thoughts far away.

"He was thinking of the sermon he had to preach on the next day, and of many other things besides, and it was a long time before it occurred to him to look around and get his bearings. When he did glance up, he saw that the forest was as thick around him as it had been when he'd started out. He was surprised, for he had ridden long enough to have reached the inhabited part of the township.

"Delsbo was about the same then as it is now. The church and parsonage and all the large farms and villages were in the northern end of the township. In the southern part were only forests and mountains. The dean realized that he had to head north to get home. There were no stars, nor was there a moon to guide him, but he felt sure that he was traveling south…or east.

"He intended to turn the horse, but hesitated. The animal had never strayed; why should he now? It was more likely that the dean was mistaken. He had been far away in thought and hadn't looked at the road, so he let the horse continue in the same direction and again lost himself in reverie.

"Suddenly a branch struck him, almost knocking him off of the horse. Then he realized that he must find out where he was. He glanced down and saw that he was riding across a soft marsh, where there was no beaten path. The horse trotted along at a brisk pace and showed no uncertainty. Again the dean had the feeling that he was going the wrong way, but because the horse was so persistent he thought that probably he was trying to find a better road, and let him go.

"The horse did very well, considering the fact that he didn't have a path to follow. He climbed the steep heights as nimbly as a goat. When they had to descend, he bunched his hooves and slid down the rocky inclines.

"'I hope he finds his way home before church is to begin,'" thought the dean uneasily. 'I wonder how the Delsbo folk would take it if I were not at church on time.'

"He didn't have to think about it too long, because he soon recognized a little creek where he had fished the summer before. He was deep in the forest, and the horse was going along toward the southeast. He seemed determined to carry the dean as far from church and rectory as he could.

"The clergyman dismounted. He couldn't let the horse carry him into the wilderness; he had to go home. Since the animal persisted in going in the wrong direction, he decided to walk and

lead him until they reached more familiar roads. The dean wound the reins around his arm and began to walk. It was not easy to hike through the forest in a heavy fur coat, but the dean was strong and wasn't afraid that he might overexert himself.

"To his dismay, the horse would not follow, but planted his hooves firmly on the ground. At last the dean was angry. He had never beaten the horse, nor did he wish to do so now, but he threw down the reins and walked away.

"'We might as well part company here, since you want to go your own way,' he said.

"He hadn't taken more than two steps before the horse went after him, took a cautious grip on his coat sleeve and stopped him. The dean looked the horse straight in the eyes, as if to learn why he acted so strangely.

"Afterward the dean could not quite understand how it was possible, but dark as it was, he plainly saw the horse's face and read it like that of a human being. He realized that the animal was afraid. The horse gave his master a look that was both imploring and reproachful.

"'I have served you day after day and done your bidding,' he seemed to say. 'Won't you follow me this one night?'

"The dean was touched by the appeal in the animal's eyes. It was clear that the horse needed his help tonight, in one way or another. Being a brave man, the dean determined to follow him. He jumped into the saddle.

"'Go on, then,' he said. 'I won't desert you. No one shall say of the dean in Delsbo that he refused to accompany someone who was in trouble.'

"He kept the reins slack and thought only of keeping his seat. It proved to be a hazardous and difficult journey—uphill most of the way. The forest was so thick that he couldn't see two feet ahead, but it seemed to him that they were going up a high mountain. The horse climbed perilous steeps. If the dean had been guiding, he wouldn't have thought of riding over such ground.

"'You don't intend to go up to Black's Ridge, do you?' laughed the dean, knowing it was one of the highest peaks in

Hälsingland. During the ride he discovered that he and the horse were not the only ones who were out that night. He heard stones roll down and branches crackle, as if animals were breaking their way through the forest. He remembered that wolves were plentiful in that area and wondered if the horse meant him well or not.

"They mounted up and up, and the higher they went the more scattered were the trees. At last they rode on almost bare highland, where the dean could look in every direction. He looked out over immeasurable tracts of land, which went up and down in mountains and valleys covered with somber forests. It was dark, but eventually he could make out where he was.

"'Why, I'm at Black's Ridge! It can't be any other mountain. There to the west I see Järv Island. To the east the sea glitters around Ag Island. Toward the north I see something shiny; it must be Dellen. Below me I see the white steam from Nian Falls. Yes, I'm up on Black's Ridge. What an adventure!'

"At the summit, the horse stopped behind a thick pine as if to hide. The dean leaned forward and pushed the branches aside so he could have an unobstructed view. The mountain's bald plate was there in front of him. It was not empty and desolate, as he had expected. In the middle of the open space was an immense boulder around which many wild animals had gathered. Apparently they were holding a secret meeting.

"Near the big rock he saw bears, so heavily built that they seemed like fur-clad blocks of stone. They were lying down, and their little eyes blinked impatiently; obviously they had come from their winter sleep to attend court, and they could hardly keep awake. Behind them, in tight rows, were hundreds of wolves. They weren't sleepy; wolves are more alert in winter than in summer. Like dogs, they sat on their haunches, whipping the ground with their tails and panting, their tongues lolling from their jaws.

"Behind the wolves the lynx skulked, stiff-legged and clumsy, like misshapen cats. They did not want to be among the other animals, and hissed and spat when one got near them. The row back of the lynx was occupied by wolverines, with dog faces and bear coats. They were unhappy on the ground, and they stamped

their pads impatiently, longing to get into the trees. Behind them, covering the entire space to the forest border, leaped foxes, weasels and martens. They were small, but they looked even more savage and bloodthirsty than the larger animals.

"All this the dean saw, for the whole place was illuminated. On the huge rock at the center was the wood nymph, who held in her hand a pine torch burning in a big, red flame. The nymph was as tall as the tallest tree in the forest. She wore a spruce-brush mantle and had spruce-cone hair. She stood very still, her face turned toward the forest—watching and listening.

"The dean saw everything as plain as plain could be, but he was too awestruck to believe what he was seeing with his own eyes. 'This can't be,' he thought. 'I have ridden much too long in the bleak forest. This must be some weird kind of optical illusion.'

"Yet he paid close attention to the spectacle, wondering what was about to happen. Before long, he heard a familiar bell sound coming from the depths of the forest. The next moment he heard footfalls and crackling branches—as when many animals break through the forest.

"A big herd of cattle was climbing the mountain. They came through the forest in the order in which they had marched to the mountain ranches. First came the bell cow, followed by the bull, then the other cows and calves. The sheep, closely herded, followed. After them came goats, and last were the horses and colts. The sheepdog trotted alongside the sheep, but neither shepherd nor shepherdess was with them.

"The dean thought it heartrending to see the tame animals coming straight toward the wild ones. He would gladly have blocked their way and called 'Halt!' but he understood that it was not within human power to stop the march of the cattle on this night, so he made no move.

"The domestic animals were afraid. If it happened to be the bell cow's turn, she advanced with drooping head and faltering step. The goats had no desire either to play or to butt. The horses tried to bear up bravely, but their bodies were quivering in fright. Most pathetic of all was the sheepdog; he kept his tail between his legs and crawled on the ground.

"The bell cow led the procession all the way up to the wood nymph, who stood on the boulder at the top of the mountain. The cow walked around the rock and then turned toward the forest without any of the wild animals touching her. In the same way all the cattle walked unmolested past the wild animals.

"As the creatures filed past, the dean saw the wood nymph lower her pine torch over one or another of them. When this happened, the beasts of prey broke into loud, exultant roars—particularly when it was lowered over a cow or some other large creature. The animal that saw the torch turning toward it uttered a cry of hopeless despair, as if a knife had been thrust into it, while the entire herd to which it belonged bellowed in sorrow.

"The dean had heard that the animals in Delsbo assembled on Black's Ridge every New Year's Eve so that the wood nymph could mark the tame animals to be prey for the wild ones. The dean pitied the poor creatures that were at the mercy of the savage beasts, when in reality they should have no master but man.

"The leading herd had just left when another bell tinkled and the cattle from another farm climbed to the mountaintop.

These came in the same order as the first and marched past the wood nymph, who stood there, solemnly marking animal after animal for death.

"Herd upon herd followed, without a break in the line of procession. Some were so small that they included only one cow and a few sheep. Others consisted of only a pair of goats. It was apparent that these were from very humble homes, but they too were compelled to pass in review.

"The dean thought of the Delsbo farmers, who loved their animals. 'If they knew what was happening, they would never allow a repetition of this!' he thought. 'They would risk their own lives rather than let their cattle be among bears and wolves, to be doomed by the wood nymph.'

"The last herd to appear was the one from the rectory farm. The dean recognized the sound of the bell from a long way off. The horse, too, must have heard it, for he began to shake.

"'So it is your turn to pass in front of the wood nymph to receive your sentence,' the dean said to the horse. 'Don't be afraid. Now I know why you brought me here, and I won't leave you.'

"The fine cattle from the parsonage farm emerged from the forest and marched to the wood nymph and the wild animals. Last in line was the horse who had brought his master. The dean stayed in the saddle, letting the animal take him to the wood nymph. He had neither knife nor gun for defense, but he had taken out the prayer book and pressed it to his heart as he exposed himself to evil.

"At first it seemed as though none had seen him. The dean's cattle filed past the wood nymph in the same order as the others had done. She did not wave the torch toward any of these, but as soon as the intelligent horse stepped forward, she made a move to mark him for death.

"Immediately the dean held up the prayer book, and the torchlight fell upon the cross on its cover. The wood nymph screamed and let the torch drop from her hand. Its flame went out.

"In the sudden transition from light to darkness, the dean

saw nothing, nor did he hear anything. About him reigned the profound stillness of a wilderness in winter.

"Then the dark clouds parted, and through the opening came the full moon to shed its light upon the ground. The dean saw that he and the horse were alone on the summit of Black's Ridge. Not one of the wild beasts was there, and the ground had not been trampled by the herds that had gone over it. The dean sat there with his prayer book in front of him, the horse under him trembling and foaming.

"By the time the dean reached home, he no longer knew whether what had happened was a dream, a vision, or reality—but he took it as a warning to remember the poor creatures who were at the mercy of wild animals. He preached so powerfully to the Delsbo peasants that in his day all the wolves and bears were exterminated from that section of the country, though they may have returned since then."

Here Bernhard ended his story. He received praise from all sides, and it seemed to be a foregone conclusion that he would get the prize. It seemed almost a pity that Clement had to compete with him.

But Clement, undaunted, began:

"One day, while I was living at Skansen, just outside of Stockholm, and longing for home—" Then he told about the tiny tomten he had ransomed so that he wouldn't have to be confined in a cage, to be stared at by people. He told, also, that no sooner had he performed this act of mercy than he was rewarded for it. He talked and talked, and the astonishment of his hearers grew greater and greater. When he came to the royal lackey and the beautiful book, the dairymaids dropped their needlework and sat staring at Clement in open-eyed wonder at his marvelous experiences.

As soon as Clement had finished, the oldest dairymaid announced that he should have the muffler. "Bernhard told what happened to someone else, but Clement has been the hero of a true story, which I consider far more important."

Everyone agreed. They saw Clement with very different eyes after hearing that he had talked with the king, and the little fiddler was afraid to show how proud he felt. At the height of his elation, however, someone asked him what had happened to the tomten.

"I didn't have time to set out the blue bowl for him myself," said Clement, "so I asked an old Laplander to do it. What has become of him since then I don't know."

No sooner had he spoken than a little pine cone struck him on the nose. It did not drop from a tree, and none of the peasants had thrown it. It was simply impossible to tell where it had come from.

"Aha, Clement," winked the dairymaid, "The tiny folk were listening. You shouldn't have left it to someone else to set out that blue bowl."

Chapter Eleven

In Medelpad

Friday, June seventeenth.
....

The boy and the eagle were out bright and early the next morning. Gorgo hoped to get far up into West Bothnia that day. As luck would have it, he heard Nils remark to himself that the people in this part of the country must be awfully poor; why, there was nothing for them to live on.

"The people here in Southern Medelpad have forests for fields," the eagle informed him.

The boy thought of the contrast between the golden rye fields with their delicate blades that grow up in one summer and the dark spruce forest with its solid trees that have to grow for many years before they're ready to be harvested.

"Making a living from a forest field must take a lot of patience," he said.

In a short while, they were over a place where the forest had been cleared and the ground was covered with stumps and lopped-off branches. The eagle heard the boy mutter to himself that it was an ugly place.

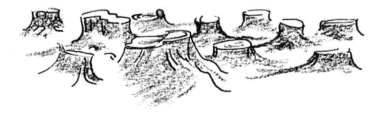

"This field was cleared last winter," the eagle said.

The boy thought of the harvesters at home, who rode on their reaping machines on summer mornings, and in a short time mowed a large field. This forest field was harvested in winter. The lumbermen went out in the wilderness when the snow was deep and the cold was most severe. It was hard work to fell even one tree. To cut down a forest like this, the men must have been out in the open for many weeks.

"Loggers must be rugged men," he said.

After two more wing strokes, they sighted a cabin at the edge of the clearing. It had no windows and only two loose boards for a door. The roof had been covered with bark and twigs, but now it was gaping, and the boy could see that inside the cabin there were only a few large stones to serve as a fireplace, and two board benches. When they were above the cabin, the eagle suspected that the boy was wondering who could have lived in the wretched hut.

"The loggers who cut down the forest field lived there," the eagle said.

The boy remembered how the reapers in his home had returned from their day's work, cheerful and happy, and how the best his mother had in the larder was always spread for them. Here, after the arduous work of the day, the loggers had to rest on hard benches in a cabin worse than an outhouse. What they had to eat he couldn't imagine.

"Are there any harvest festivals for these laborers?" he questioned.

Farther on they saw a road winding through the forest. It was narrow and zigzagging, hilly and stony, and cut up by brooks. As they flew over it, the eagle knew that the boy was wondering what was hauled over the road.

"On this road the lumber was taken to the stack," the eagle said.

The boy remembered the fun they had at home when the harvest wagons drawn by two sturdy horses carried the grain from the field. The man who drove sat proudly on top of the load. The horses danced and pricked up their ears, and the village children, who were allowed to climb on the sheaves, sat there laughing and shouting, half-pleased, half-frightened. The logs were drawn up and down steep hills. The horses and their drivers must have been worked to their limit and been in peril on many occasions.

"I'm afraid there has been very little happiness along this road," the boy observed.

The eagle flew on, and soon they were over a riverbank covered with logs, chips and bark. Nils wondered why it looked so littered.

"Logs have been stacked here," the eagle told him.

The boy thought of how the grain stacks in his part of the country were piled close to the farms, as if they were their greatest ornaments, while here the harvest was borne to a desolate river strand and left there.

"I wonder if anyone out in this wilderness counts his stacks and compares them with his neighbor's," he said.

A little later they flew over Ljungen, a river which glides through a broad valley. Everything was so different that they might well have thought they had crossed into another country. The dark spruce forest had stopped on the inclines above the valley, and the slopes were dressed in light-stemmed birches and aspens. The valley was so broad that in many places the river widened into lakes. Along the shores lay a large, flourishing town.

As they soared above the valley, the boy wondered how the fields and meadows could provide a living for so many people.

"The loggers who cut the forest live here," the eagle said.

The boy was thinking of the humble cabins and hedged-in farms down in Skåne when he said, "Why, here the peasants live in real manors. Maybe it is worthwhile to work in the forest after all."

The eagle had intended to travel straight north, but when he had flown out over the river, the boy wanted to know who handled the timber after it was stacked on the riverbank. Nils remembered how careful the people at home were; they didn't want a single grain to be wasted. Here were rafts of logs floating down the river, ignored. He could not believe that more than half of the logs ever reached their final destination.

Many were floating in midstream; for them all went smoothly. Others moved close to shore, bumping against points of land, and some were left behind in the still waters of the

creeks. There were so many logs on the lakes that they covered the surface of the water; these logs appeared to be lodged indefinitely. At the bridges they stuck; in the falls they were bunched, then pyramided and broken in two. Afterward, in the rapids, they were blocked by the stones and massed into heaps.

"I wonder how long it takes for the logs to get to the mills," said the boy.

The eagle continued his slow flight down River Ljungen. Over many places he paused in the air on outspread wings so that the boy could see how this harvest work was done.

When they saw some loggers at work, the eagle said, "They take care of the late harvesting."

The boy remembered the perfect ease with which the people at home had driven their grain to the mill. Here the men ran along the shores with long boat hooks, and only with great effort urged the logs along. They waded into the river and were soaked from head to toe. They jumped from stone to stone far out into the rapids, and walked on rolling logs as calmly as though they were on flat ground. They were daring men.

"They remind me of the iron molders in the mining districts, who juggle fire as if it were perfectly harmless," remarked the boy. "The loggers play with water as if they were its masters; they seem to have subjugated it so that it cannot harm them."

Eventually they neared the mouth of the river, and Bothnia Bay was beyond them. Gorgo turned north along the coast. Before they had traveled very far, they saw a lumber camp as large as a small city. As the eagle circled back and forth above it, he heard the boy remark that this place looked interesting.

"It's the Svartvik lumber camp," the eagle said.

The boy thought of the mill at home, which stood peacefully covered in foliage and moved its wings very slowly. This mill, where they ground the forest harvest, stood on the water. The mill pond was crowded with logs. One by one the helpers seized them with their cant hooks, crowded them into chutes and hurried them along to whirling saws.

What happened to the logs inside, the boy could not see, but he heard loud buzzing and roaring, and from the other end of the house small cars ran out, loaded with white planks. The cars ran on shining tracks down to the lumberyard, where planks were piled in rows, forming streets—like blocks of houses in a city. In one place they were building new piles; in another they were pulling down old ones. These were carried aboard two large ships which lay waiting for cargo. The place was busy with workmen, and in the woods, back of the yard, they had their homes.

"The way they work here, they'll soon saw up all the forests in Medelpad," said the boy.

The eagle moved his wings just a little and carried the boy above another large camp, much like the first—with the mill, yard, wharf, and the homes of the workmen.

"This is called Kubikenborg," the eagle said.

He flapped his wings slowly, flew past two big lumber camps and approached a large city. When the eagle heard the boy ask what it was called, he cried: "This is Sundsvall, the manor of the lumber districts."

The boy remembered the cities of Skåne, which looked so old and gray and solemn. Here in the bleak north, the city of Sundsvall faced a beautiful bay, and looked young and happy and beaming. There was something odd about the city when one saw it from above. In the middle stood a cluster of tall stone structures which looked so imposing that their match was hardly to be found in Stockholm. Around the stone buildings was a large open space. Then came a wreath of frame houses, which looked pretty and cozy in their little gardens, but they seemed to be conscious of the fact that they were much poorer than the stone houses and dared not go into their neighborhood.

"This must be a wealthy and powerful city," remarked the boy. "Can it be possible that the forest soil is the source of all this?"

The eagle flapped his wings again and cruised to Aln Island, which lies opposite from Sundsvall. The boy was surprised to see all the sawmills along the shores. On Aln Island the sawmills stood one next to another, and on the mainland opposite were mill upon mill, lumberyard upon lumberyard. He counted forty at least but believed there were many more.

"How wonderful it all looks from up here," he marveled. "I haven't seen this much life and activity on the whole trip. We live in a great country. Wherever I go, there is always some way for people to make a living."

THE TRAVELS OF
BOOK TWO
NILS HOLGERSSON

Chapter Twelve

A Morning in Ångermanland

The Bread

....

Saturday, June eighteenth.

The next morning, when the eagle had flown some distance into Ångermanland, he remarked that this time he was the one who was hungry and must find something to eat. He set the boy down in an enormous pine on a high mountain ridge, and away he flew.

The boy found a comfortable seat in a cleft branch and looked out over Ångermanland. It was a beautiful morning. Sunshine gilded the treetops, a soft breeze played in the pine needles, and the sweetest fragrance was wafted through the forest. The boy felt carefree and happy.

He had a perfect view in every direction. The country west of him was all peaks and tableland, and the farther away they were, the higher and wilder they appeared. To the east there were also many peaks, but these sank lower and lower toward the sea, where the land became flat. Everywhere he saw shining rivers and brooks, which were having a troublesome journey with rapids and falls as long as they ran between mountains, but spread out clear and wide as they neared the coast. Bothnia Bay was dotted with islands and notched with points, but farther out was open, blue water, like the summer sky.

When the boy had had enough of looking at the landscape, he untied his knapsack, took out a piece of fine, white bread, and began to eat.

"I don't think I have ever tasted such good bread," thought he, "and I have so much left! There's enough to last me for a couple of days." As he munched, he mused on how he had gotten the bread. "It must be because I got it in such a nice way that it tastes so good to me."

The golden eagle had left Medelpad the evening before. He had hardly crossed the border into Ångermanland when the boy caught a glimpse of a fertile valley and a river that surpassed anything of the kind he had seen before.

As the boy looked down at the rich valley, he complained of feeling hungry. He had had no food for two days, he said, and now he was famished. Gorgo didn't want it said that the boy had fared worse in his company than when he traveled with the wild geese, so he slackened his speed.

"Why haven't you said something before now? You shall have all the food you want. There's no need to starve when you have an eagle for a traveling companion."

Just then the eagle sighted a farmer who was sowing a field near the river strand. The man carried seeds in a basket hung from his neck, and each time it was emptied he refilled it from a seed sack that stood at the end of the furrow. The eagle reasoned that the sack must be filled with the best food the boy could wish for, so he darted toward it.

Before he could get there, however, a terrible clamor arose around him. Sparrows, crows and swallows came rushing up with wild screams, thinking that the eagle meant to swoop down on some poor bird.

A Morning in Ångermanland

"Away, away, robber! Away, away, bird killer!" they cried. They made such a racket that it attracted the farmer, who came running, so that Gorgo had to flee, and the boy didn't get any seed.

The small birds acted in the most extraordinary manner. Not only did they force the eagle to flee, they pursued him down the valley, and everywhere the people heard their cries. Women came out and clapped their hands so loud that it sounded like musket volleys. Men rushed out with rifles.

The same thing was repeated every time the eagle swept toward the ground, and the boy gave up any hope that the eagle could get food for him. It had never occurred to him that Gorgo was so hated. He almost pitied him.

In a little while they reached a homestead where a housewife had just been baking. She had set a platter of sugared buns in the backyard to cool and was standing beside it, watching, so that the cat and dog would not steal the buns.

The eagle circled down to the yard but didn't dare alight right under the eyes of the peasant woman. He flew up and down, unsure of what to do. Twice he came down as far as the chimney, then rose again.

The peasant woman watched the eagle. "How strangely he acts," she thought. "I believe he wants one of my buns."

She was a beautiful woman—tall and fair, with a cheery look about her. Laughing heartily, she took a bun from the platter and held it above her head.

"If you want it, come and take it," she challenged.

Although the eagle did not understand her language, he knew at once that she was offering him the bun. With lightning speed, he swooped to the bread, snatched it and flew upward to the heights.

When the boy saw the eagle snatch the bread, he wept for joy—not because he would escape hunger for a few days, but because he was touched by the peasant woman's sharing her bread with a savage bird of prey.

Where he now sat on the pine branch he could recall what the woman looked like as she stood in the yard and held up the bread. She must have known that the large bird was a golden eagle—a plunderer, who was usually welcomed with gunshots. No doubt she had also seen the odd little tomten he bore on his back. What they were didn't matter to her. When she realized that they were hungry, she generously shared her good bread with them.

"If I ever become human again," thought the boy, "I shall look up the pretty woman who lives near the great river and thank her for her kindness to us."

While the boy was still eating breakfast, he smelled a faint odor of smoke coming from the north. He turned and saw a tiny spiral, white as a mist, rise from a forest ridge—not from the one nearest him, but from the one beyond it. It was odd to see smoke in the wild forest, but it might be that a mountain stock farm lay over yonder, and the women were boiling their morning coffee.

The smoke increased and spread. It could not come from a ranch, but perhaps there were charcoal kilns in the forest. The smoke increased every moment. Now it curled over the whole mountaintop. A charcoal kiln couldn't possibly produce that much smoke. There must be a destructive fire of some sort, for many birds flew over to the nearest ridge. Hawks, grouse and other birds, who were so small that it was impossible to recognize them from a distance, fled from the fire.

The tiny white spiral of smoke grew into a thick, white cloud, rolled over the edge of the ridge and sank toward the valley. Sparks and flakes of soot shot up from the clouds, and in many places one could see a red flame in the smoke. A big fire was raging over there, but what was burning? Surely there was no large farm hidden in the forest.

The source of the fire must be more than a farm. Now the smoke came not only from the ridge, but from the valley below it, which the boy could not see because the next ridge obstructed his view. Huge clouds of smoke ascended. The forest was on fire!

It was difficult for him to grasp the idea that the fresh, green pines could burn. If it really were the forest that was burning, the fire might spread all the way over to him. It seemed improbable, but he wished the eagle would return. It would be best to be away from here. The mere smell of the smoke which he drew in with every breath was a torture.

All at once he heard a terrible crackling and sputtering. It came from the ridge nearest him. There, on the highest point, stood a tall pine like the one in which he sat. A moment before it had been a gorgeous red in the morning light. Now all the needles flashed, and the pine caught fire. Never before had it looked so beautiful.

This was the last time it could exhibit any beauty, for the pine was the first tree on the ridge to burn. It was impossible to tell how the flames had reached it. Had the fire flown on red wings or crawled along the ground like a snake? It wasn't easy to say, but there it was. The pine burned like a birch seedling.

Ah, look! Now smoke curled up in many places on the ridge. The forest fire was both bird and snake; it could fly in the air over wide stretches or steal along the ground. The whole ridge was ablaze.

A hasty flight of birds circled up through the smoke like flakes of soot. They flew across the valley and came to the ridge where the boy sat. A horned owl perched beside him, and on a

branch just above him a hen hawk alighted. These would have been dangerous neighbors any other time, but now they did not even glance in his direction—only stared at the fire. Probably they could not make out what was wrong with the forest.

A marten ran up the pine to the tip of a branch and looked at the burning heights. Close beside the marten sat a squirrel, but they didn't appear to notice each other.

The fire came rushing down the slope, hissing and roaring like a tornado. Through the smoke one could see the flames dart from tree to tree. Before a branch caught fire, it was enveloped in a thin veil of smoke. Then all the needles grew red, and it began to crackle and blaze.

In the glen below ran a little brook bordered by elms and small birches. It appeared as if the flames would halt there. Leafy trees are not as ready to take fire as fir trees. The fire did pause as if before a gate that could stop it. It glowed and crackled and tried to leap across the brook to the pine woods on the other side, but could not reach them.

For a short time the fire was restrained, but then it shot a long flame over to the large, dry pine that stood on the slope, and this was soon ablaze. The fire had crossed the brook! The heat was so intense that every tree on the mountain was ready to burn. With the roar and rush of the maddest storm and the wildest torrent, the forest fire flew over to the ridge.

Then the hawk and the owl rose, and the marten dashed down the tree. In a few seconds more the fire would reach the top of the pine, and the boy, too, would have to move. It was not easy to slide down the long, straight pine trunk. He took as firm a hold of it as he could and slid in long stretches between the knotty branches. Finally he tumbled headlong to the ground. He had no time to find out if he was hurt—only to hurry away. The fire raced down the pine like a raging tempest. The ground under his feet was hot and smoldering. On either side of him ran a lynx and an adder, and right beside the snake fluttered a mother grouse who was hurrying along with her little downy chicks.

When the refugees descended the mountain to the glen, they met people fighting the fire. They had been there for some time, but the boy had been gazing so intently in the direction of the fire that he had not noticed them before.

In this glen was a brook bordered by a row of leaf trees, and behind these trees the people worked. They felled the fir trees nearest the elms, scooped water from the brook and poured it over the ground, washing away heather and myrtle to prevent the fire from stealing up to the birch brush.

They, too, thought only of the fire that was rushing toward them. None of the fleeing animals attracted their attention. No one struck at the adder or tried to catch the mother grouse as she ran back and forth with her little peeping chicks. They did not even bother about Thumbietot. In their hands they held large, charred pine branches that had dropped into the brook—as if they intended to challenge the fire with these weapons. There were not many men, and it was strange to see them stand there fighting the flames when all other living creatures were fleeing.

A Morning in Ångermanland

As the fire came roaring and rushing down the slope with its intolerable heat and suffocating smoke, ready to hurl itself over brook and leaf-tree wall to reach the opposite shore, the people drew away as if unable to withstand it. Then they turned back to fight again.

The fire raged, sparks poured like a rain of fire over the leaf trees, and long tongues of flame shot hissingly out from the smoke as if the forest on the other side were sucking them in.

The men stayed behind the leaf-tree wall. When the ground began to smolder, they brought water in containers and dampened it. When a tree became wreathed in smoke, they felled it at once, pushed it down and put out the flames. Where the fire crept along the heather, they beat it with wet pine branches and smothered it.

By now the smoke enveloped everything. One could not possibly see how the battle was going, but it was easy enough to understand that it was a hard fight and that several times the fire came near penetrating farther.

After awhile the loud roar of the flames decreased, and the smoke cleared. By then the leaf trees had lost all of their foliage, the ground under them was charred, the faces of the men were blackened by smoke and dripping with sweat...but the forest fire was conquered. It had ceased to flame up. Soft white smoke crept along the ground, and from it peeped out a lot of black stumps. This was all there was left of the beautiful forest.

The boy scrambled onto a rock to see how the fire had been quenched, but now that the forest was safe again, his peril began. The owl and the hawk simultaneously turned their eyes toward him.

Just then he heard a familiar voice calling to him. Gorgo, the golden eagle, came sweeping through the forest, and soon the boy was soaring among the clouds—rescued from every peril.

Chapter Thirteen

Västerbotten and Lapland

The Five Scouts

One time, at Skansen, the boy had sat under the steps at Bollnäs cottage and overheard Clement Larsson and the old Laplander talk about Norrland. The men agreed that it was the most beautiful part of Sweden. Clement, however, thought that the southern part was the best, while the Laplander preferred the northern part.

As they argued, it became clear that Clement had never been farther north than Härnösand. The Laplander laughed at him for speaking so confidently about places he had never seen.

"Let me tell you a story, Clement, to give you some idea of what Lapland is like, since you haven't seen it," he volunteered.

"I'm always willing to listen to a good story," answered Clement, and the old Laplander began:

"It once happened that the birds who lived down in Sweden, south of Sameland, felt overcrowded and thought of moving north. They gathered to discuss the matter. The young and eager birds wanted to start at once, but the older and wiser ones passed a resolution to send scouts to explore the new country.

"'Let each of the five major bird families send out a scout,' said the old and wise birds, 'to find out if there is enough room for all of us—food and hiding places.'

"Five intelligent and capable birds were immediately appointed by the five major bird families. The forest birds selected a grouse, the field birds a lark, the seabirds a gull, the freshwater birds a loon, and the cliff birds a snow sparrow.

"When the five chosen ones were ready to start, the grouse, who was the largest and most commanding, said: 'There are huge stretches of land ahead. If we travel together, it will take a long time for us to cover all of the territory we must explore. If, on the other hand, we travel singly—each one exploring his special portion of the country—the whole expedition can be accomplished within a few days.'

"The other scouts thought his suggestion was a good one and agreed to follow it. It was decided that the grouse should explore the midlands. The lark was to travel east and the sea gull still farther east, where the land bordered on the sea. The loon should fly over the territory west of the midlands and the snow sparrow to the extreme west.

"In accordance with this plan, the five birds flew over the whole northland. Then they returned and told the assembly of birds what they had discovered.

"The gull, who had traveled along the seacoast, spoke first. 'The north is a fine place,' he said. 'The sounds are full of fish, and there are endless points and islands. Most of these are uninhabited, and the birds will find plenty of room there. The humans do a little fishing and sailing in the sounds, but not enough to disturb us. If the seabirds follow my advice, they will move north immediately.'

"When the gull had finished, the lark, who had explored the land back from the coast, spoke up. 'I don't know what the gull means by islands and points,' the lark said. 'I have traveled over huge fields and flowery meadows. I have never seen a country like it. It's crossed by large streams; their shores are dotted with homesteads, and at the mouth of the rivers are cities. For the most part, though, the country is uninhabited by humans. If the field birds follow my advice, they will move north immediately.'

"After the lark came the grouse, who had flown over the midlands. 'I don't know what the lark means by meadows, nor do I know what the sea gull means by islands and points,' said he. 'I have seen only pine forests on this whole trip. There are also rushing streams and stretches of moss-grown swampland, but what is not river or swamp is forest. If the forest birds follow my advice, they will move north immediately.'

"After the grouse came the loon, who had explored the borderland to the west. 'I don't know what the grouse means by forests, nor do I know where the eyes of the lark and the gull could have been,' remarked the loon. 'There's hardly any land up there—only big lakes. Beautiful shores surround glistening blue mountain lakes, which pour into roaring waterfalls. If the freshwater birds follow my advice, they will move north immediately.'

"The last speaker was the snow sparrow, who had flown along the western boundary. 'I have no idea what the loon means by lakes, nor do I know where the grouse, the lark and the gull have been,' he said. 'I found one vast, mountainous region up north. I didn't run across any fields or pine forests, but peak after peak and highlands. I have seen ice fields, snow and mountain brooks with water as white as milk. No farmers, cattle nor homesteads have I seen, but only Lapps and reindeer and huts. If the cliff birds follow my advice, they will move north immediately.'

"When the five scouts had presented their reports to the assembly, they began to call one another liars. The old and wise birds, however, listened to their accounts with joy and calmed the scouts.

"'Don't quarrel,' they said. 'We understand from your reports that up north there are large mountain tracts, a big lake region, tremendous forest lands, a wide plain, and a group of islands. This is more than we could have expected—more than many a mighty kingdom can boast within its borders.'"

The Moving Landscape

Saturday, June eighteenth.

The boy had been reminded of the old Laplander's story because he was now traveling over the country of which the man had spoken. The eagle told him that the coast spread beneath them was Västerbotten and that the blue ridges far to the west were in Lapland.

Just to be seated comfortably on Gorgo's back, after all he had suffered in the forest fire, was a real relief. Besides, they were having a fine trip. The flight was so easy that sometimes it seemed as if they were standing still in the air, yet everything under them was in motion. The whole earth and everything on it moved slowly southward. The forest, the fields, the fences, the rivers, the cities, the islands, the sawmills—all were on the march. The boy wondered where they intended to go. Had they grown tired of being so far north and wished to move south?

Only one thing stood still, and that was a railway train. Like Gorgo, it could not move from the spot. The locomotive spewed smoke and sparks, and the clatter of the wheels could be heard all the way up to the boy. Still it seemed to be at a complete stop. Forests rushed by, the flag station rushed by, fences and telegraph poles rushed by, but the train stood still. A broad river with a long bridge came toward it, but the river and the bridge glided along under the train with perfect ease.

Finally a railway station appeared. The stationmaster stood

on the platform with his red flag and moved slowly toward the train. When he waved his little flag, the locomotive belched even darker smoke curls than before and whistled mournfully because it had to come to a halt. All of a sudden it began to move toward the south, like everything else. The boy saw all the coach doors open and the passengers step out while both cars and people were moving southward.

He glanced away from the earth and tried to look straight ahead. Staring at the curious little train had made him dizzy, but after he had gazed for a moment at a little white cloud, he looked down again—thinking all the while that Gorgo and he were quite still and everything else was traveling south. What if the grainfield running along under him, which must have been newly sown—for he had seen a green blade on it—were to travel all the way down to Skåne where the rye was in full bloom at this season? Imagine that!

Up here the pine forests were very different. The trees were bare, the branches short, and the needles were almost black. Many trees were bald at the top and looked sickly. If a forest like that were to journey down to Kolmården and see a real forest, how inferior it would feel!

The gardens he now saw had some bushes, but no fruit trees or lindens or chestnut trees—only mountain ash and birch. There were some vegetable beds, but they were not yet hoed or planted. If such an excuse for a garden were to come trailing into Sörmland, the province of gardens, it would think itself a poor wilderness by comparison.

Imagine an immense plain, like the one now gliding beneath him, coming under the very eyes of the poor Småland peasants. They would hurry away from their meager garden plots and stony fields to begin plowing and sowing.

There was one thing, however, of which this north country had more of than anywhere else—light. Night must have set in, because the cranes stood sleeping in the marshland, but it was as light as day. Unlike everything else, the sun had not traveled south. Instead, it had gone so far north that it shone in the boy's face. It seemed to have no notion at all of setting that night.

If only this light and this sun were shining on West Vemmenhög! It would certainly please the boy's father and mother to have a working day that lasted twenty-four hours.

The Dream

Sunday, June nineteenth.

The boy raised his head and looked around, bewildered. He'd been sleeping in some place where he had not been before. No, he had never seen this glen nor the mountains round about, and never had he seen such weak and stunted birches as those under which he now lay.

Where was the eagle? The boy could see no sign of him. Had Gorgo deserted him? Well, then here was another adventure.

The boy lay down again, closed his eyes and tried to recall the circumstances under which he had fallen asleep. He remembered that as long as he was traveling over Västerbotten he had imagined that the eagle and he had stopped in midair and that the land under them was moving southward. As the eagle turned northwest, the wind had come from that side, and again he had felt a current of air, so that the land below stopped moving and the eagle seemed to carry him onward with terrific speed.

"We're flying into Lapland," Gorgo had said, and the boy had leaned forward to see the country of which he had heard so much. The boy had felt somewhat disappointed at not seeing anything but tracts of forest land and wide marshes. Forest followed marsh, and marsh followed forest. The monotony finally made him so sleepy that he had almost fallen to the ground.

He told the eagle that he could not stay on his back another minute, but must sleep. Gorgo had promptly swooped to the ground, where the boy had dropped down onto a moss tuft. Then Gorgo put a talon around him and soared into the air with him.

"Sleep, Thumbietot," he said. "The sunshine keeps me awake, and I want to continue the journey."

Although the boy hung in this uncomfortable position, he

dozed and dreamed. In his dream, he was on a broad road in southern Sweden, hurrying along as fast as his little legs could carry him. He was not alone; many wayfarers were hiking in the same direction. Close beside him marched grain-filled rye blades, blossoming cornflowers and yellow daisies. Heavily laden apple trees went puffing along, followed by vine-covered beanstalks, big clusters of white daisies and bunches of berry bushes. Tall beeches, oaks and lindens strolled leisurely in the middle of the road, their branches swaying, and they stepped aside for no one. Between the boy's feet darted little flowers—wild strawberry blossoms, white anemones, clover and forget-me-nots.

At first he thought that only the vegetable family was on the move, but soon he saw that animals and people accompanied them. Insects were buzzing around advancing bushes, fishes were swimming in moving ditches, birds were singing in strolling trees. Both tame and wild animals were racing, and they were accompanied by people—some with spades and scythes, others with axes, and yet others with fishing nets.

The procession marched gaily along, and the boy wasn't surprised by that when he saw who was leading it. The sun itself was at the head of the column; it rolled on like a great shining head—with hair of many-colored rays and a face beaming with merriment and kindliness.

"Forward, march!" it kept calling out. "No one need be afraid when I am here. Forward, march!"

"Where does the sun want to take us?" asked the boy. A rye blade walking beside him said, "He's leading us up to Lapland to fight the ice witch."

The boy noticed that some of the travelers hesitated. Then they slowed down and finally stopped. The roebuck and the wheat blade were lingering by the wayside; so were the blackberry bush, the little yellow buttercup, the chestnut tree and the grouse.

He looked around him and tried to figure out why so many stopped. Then he realized that they were no longer in southern Sweden. They had marched so fast that they were already in Svealand.

Up there the oak began to move more cautiously. It paused awhile to consider, took a few faltering steps, then stopped.

"What's wrong with the oak?" asked the boy.

"It's afraid of the ice witch," said a fair young birch that went along so boldly and cheerfully that it was fun to watch it. The crowd hurried on. In a short time they were in Norrland, and now it didn't matter how much the sun cried and coaxed; the apple tree stopped, the cherry tree stopped, the rye blade stopped.

The boy asked them, "What's the matter? Why are you deserting the sun?"

"We're afraid of the ice witch, who lives in Lapland," they replied.

The procession was, by now, far north. The rye blade, the barley, the wild strawberry, the blueberry bush, the pea stalk and the currant bush had come as far as this. The elk and the domestic cow had been walking side by side, but now they stopped. The sun no doubt would have been almost deserted if new followers had not happened along. Osier bushes and a lot of brushy vegetation joined the procession. Laps and reindeer, mountain owl, mountain fox and willow grouse followed.

Then the boy heard something coming toward them—mighty rivers and creeks sweeping along.

"Why are they in such a hurry?" he asked.

"They are fleeing from the ice witch, who lives in the mountains."

All of a sudden the boy saw a high, dark, turreted wall in front of him. Instantly the sun turned its beaming face toward the wall and flooded it with light. Magically the wall disappeared, and the most glorious mountains loomed up—one behind another. Their peaks were rose-colored in the sunlight, their slopes azure and gold-tinted.

"Onward, onward!" urged the sun as it climbed the steep cliffs. "There's no danger as long as I am with you."

Halfway up, the bold young birch deserted, also the sturdy pine and the persistent spruce. There, too, the Laplander and the willow brush deserted. At last, when the sun reached the top of the mountain, there was no one with it except Nils Holgersson.

The sun rolled into a cave, where the walls were covered with ice, and Nils wanted to follow, but he was afraid to go any farther than the opening of the cave. In there he saw something dreadful. Far back in the cave sat an old witch with an ice body, hair of icicles and a mantle of snow. At her feet lay three black wolves, who rose and opened their jaws when the sun approached. From the mouth of one came a penetrating cold, from the second a wild north wind, and from the third came darkness.

"That must be the ice witch and her tribe," thought the boy. He knew he should run away, but he wanted to see the outcome of the meeting between the sun and the ice witch, so he waited.

The ice witch did not move—only turned her hideous face toward the sun. It appeared to the boy that she was beginning to sigh and tremble. Her snow mantle fell, and the three ferocious wolves howled less savagely.

Suddenly the sun cried, "My time is up!" and rolled back out of the cave.

The ice witch let loose her three wolves, and instantly the north wind, cold and darkness rushed from the cave, chasing the sun.

"Drive him out! Drive him back!" screamed the ice witch. "Chase him so far that he can never come back! Teach him that Lapland is mine!"

Nils was so unhappy when he saw that the sun might be driven from Lapland that he awakened with a cry. When he recovered his senses, he realized that he was at the bottom of a ravine.

Where was Gorgo? Nils got up and looked around. Then he happened to look up and saw a peculiar structure of pine twigs and branches on a cliff ledge.

"This must be one of those eagle nests that Gorgo—" He tore off his cap, waved it in the air and shouted. This was the glen where the wild geese lived in the summer, and on the cliff above was Gorgo's nest. He had arrived. He would see Morton

Goosey-Gander and Akka and all the other comrades.
"Hurray!"

The Meeting

The glen was quiet. The sun had not yet risen above the cliffs, and Nils Holgersson knew that it was too early in the morning for the geese to be awake.

The boy walked along leisurely as he looked for his friends. Before he had gone very far, he paused with a smile; he saw such a pretty sight. A wild goose was sleeping in a neat little nest, and beside her stood her goosey-gander. He slept too, but it was obvious that he had stationed himself near her to be ready for danger.

The boy went on without disturbing them and peered through the willow brush. He saw another goose couple. These were strangers, not of his flock, but he was so happy that he began to hum—just because he had come across wild geese.

He looked into another bit of brushwood, and there at last he saw two that were familiar. It was certainly Neljä nesting there, and the goosey-gander beside her was surely Kolme. Why, of course! The boy would have liked to awaken them, but he let them sleep on, and walked away.

In the next brush he found Viisi and Kuusi, and not far from them he saw Yksi and Kaksi. All four were asleep, and the boy went by without disturbing them.

As he approached another brush, he thought he saw something white shimmering among the bushes, and his heart thumped with joy. The dainty Dunfin sat on an egg-filled nest, and beside her stood her white goosey-gander. Although he slept, it was easy to see how proud he was to watch over his wife up here among the Lapland mountains. The boy did not care to waken the goosey-gander, so he walked on.

He had to look a long time before he came across any more wild geese. Then, on a little hill, he saw something that resembled a small, gray moss tuft, and he knew that he had found Akka from Kebnekaise. She stood, wide awake, looking about as if she were keeping watch over the whole glen.

"Good morning, Mother Akka," said the boy. "Please don't waken the other geese yet. I'd like to talk with you in private."

The old leader goose came rushing down the hill and up to the boy. She seized him and shook him, and then she stroked him with her bill before she shook him again. Not one word did she say, though, since he asked her not to waken the others.

Thumbietot kissed Akka on both cheeks and then related how he had been carried off to Skansen and held captive.

"Smirre Fox, minus one of his ears, also sat imprisoned in the foxes' cage at Skansen," said the boy. "Although he was mean to us, I couldn't help feeling sorry for him; he looked so dejected.

"I made some good friends at Skansen, and one day I learned from the Lapp dog that a man had come to Skansen to buy foxes. He was from some island far out in the ocean. All the foxes had been exterminated there, and the rats were about to get the better of the inhabitants, so they wanted the foxes back again.

"As soon as I learned of this, I went to Smirre's cage and said to him: 'Tomorrow some men are coming here to get a pair of foxes. Don't hide, Smirre. Stay in the front of the cage and make sure that you are chosen. Then you will be free again.'

"He did what I said, and now he is running free on the island. What do you think, Mother Akka? If you had been in my place, wouldn't you have done the same thing?"

"You have acted in a way that makes me wish I had done that myself," said the leader goose proudly.

"It's a relief to know that you approve," said the boy. "There is one more thing I need to ask you about.

"One day I happened to see Gorgo, the eagle—the one who fought with Morton Goosey-Gander. He was a prisoner at Skansen too, and he looked pitifully forlorn. I thought about filing the wire roof of the cage and letting him out, but I also considered his being a dangerous robber and a bird eater. I wondered if it wouldn't be better to let him stay where he was. What do you think, Mother Akka? Was it right to think that way?"

"No, it was not right!" retorted Akka. "Say what you will about the eagles, they are proud birds and greater lovers of freedom than all others. It's wrong to keep them in captivity. As soon as you are rested, let's make the trip together to liberate Gorgo."

"That is just what I expected from you, Mother Akka," replied the boy eagerly. "Some say you no longer have any love in your heart for the one you reared so tenderly, because he lives as eagles live. I know now that it isn't true.

"I'll see if Morton Goosey-Gander is awake. Meanwhile, if you would like to thank the one who brought me back to you, I think you'll find him up there on the cliff ledge, where once you found a helpless eaglet."

THE TRAVELS OF
BOOK TWO
NILS HOLGERSSON

Chapter Fourteen

Osa, the Goose Girl, and Little Mats

The year that Nils Holgersson traveled with the wild geese, everyone was talking about two little children, a boy and a girl, who were hiking through the country. They were from Sunnerbo township, in Småland, and had once lived with their parents and four brothers and sisters in a little cabin on the heath.

While the two children, Osa and Mats, were still small, a homeless woman came to their cabin one night and begged for shelter. Although the place could hardly hold the family, she was taken in. During the night, the poor woman coughed so hard that the children imagined that the house shook. By morning she was too sick to leave. The children's father and mother were as kind to her as they could be. They gave up their bed to her and slept on the floor, while the father went to the doctor and brought her medicine.

For the first few days, the sick woman demanded constant attention and never said a word of thanks. Later she became quiet and finally asked to be carried out to the heath and left there to die.

When her hosts would not do this, she told them that for the last few years she had roamed with a band of gypsies. She herself was not of gypsy blood, but was the daughter of a well-to-do farmer. She had run away from home and gone with the nomads. She believed that a gypsy woman who was angry with her had brought this sickness upon her. Nor was that all. The gypsy woman had also cursed her, saying that all who took her under their roof or were kind to her would suffer a like fate. She believed this and therefore begged them to throw her out of the house. She did not want to bring misfortune upon such good people. The peasants still refused to do what she said. They may have been alarmed, but they wouldn't turn out a poor, sick person.

Soon after that she died, and then came one tragedy after another. Before, there had never been anything but happiness in that cabin. The family was poor...yet not so awfully poor. The father was a maker of weaver's combs, and the family helped him with the work. He made the frames, and his wife and the older children did the binding, while the smaller ones planed the teeth and cut them out.

They worked from morning until night, but the time passed pleasantly, especially when the father talked of the days when he traveled in foreign lands and sold the weaver's combs. He made so many funny quips and jokes that sometimes his wife and children laughed until their sides ached.

The weeks following the death of the homeless woman lingered in the minds of the children like a horrible nightmare. Whether the time was long or short, they couldn't recall, but they did remember that they were always having funerals at home. Their brothers and sisters died, one after another, and it was very quiet and sad in the cabin.

The mother kept up a measure of courage, but the father was not a bit like himself. He could no longer work nor laugh, but sat from morning till night, his head buried in his hands.

Once—that was after the third burial—the father had broken out into wild talk, which frightened the children. He said that he could not understand why such a curse could come upon them. Helping the sick woman was a good deed. Could it be true, then, that the evil in this world was more powerful than the good? His wife tried to reason with him, but couldn't.

A few days later the eldest child became ill. She had always
been the father's favorite. When he realized that she, too, would die, he fled from all the misery. The mother never said anything, but she thought it was best for him to be away. Perhaps otherwise he would lose his reason. He had brooded too long over the idea that God had allowed a wicked person to cause so much evil.

After the father went away, they became very poor. For a while he sent them money, but then the money stopped.

On the day of the eldest child's burial, the mother closed the cabin and left home with the two remaining children, Osa and Mats. She went down to Skåne to work in the beet fields, and there she found a job at the Jordberga sugar refinery. She was a good worker and had a cheerful and generous nature. Everyone liked her. People were amazed at her composure, considering what she had suffered, but the mother was strong and patient. When anyone asked her about her two children, she only said, "I will soon lose them, too," without a quaver in her voice or a tear in her eye. She was accustomed to hardship and sorrow.

It did not turn out the way she had thought, though. She was the one who became ill. She'd gone to Skåne in the beginning of the summer; before autumn she was gone, and the children were alone.

While their mother was ill, she had often told them that she never regretted having let the sick woman stay with them. It was not hard to die when one had done right, she said, for then one could leave this life with a clear conscience.

Before the mother passed away, she tried to make some provision for her children. She asked the people with whom she lived to let them remain in the room which she had occupied. If the children had shelter, they would not become a burden to anyone. She knew they could take care of themselves.

Osa and Mats were allowed to keep the room on condition that they would tend geese, since it was always hard to find children willing to do that kind of work. True to the mother's word, the two did take care of themselves. The girl made candy, and the boy carved wooden toys, which they sold at the farmhouses. They had a talent for buying and selling, and soon began buying eggs and butter from the farmers, which they sold to the workers at the sugar refinery.

Osa was the older of the two, and by the time she was thirteen, she was as responsible as a grown woman. She was a serious girl. Mats was the opposite—lively and talkative. His sister used to say that he could out-cackle the geese.

One evening, after the children had been at Jordberga for two years, a lecture was held at the schoolhouse. Evidently it was meant for grownups, but the two Småland children were in the audience. They did not think of themselves as children, and few other people thought of them that way either. The lecturer talked about the dreadful disease called the White Plague, which carried off so many people in Sweden every year. He spoke in simple terms, and the children understood every word.

After the lecture, they waited outside the school building. When the lecturer came out, they walked up and asked if they might talk with him. The stranger must have wondered at the two little children standing there talking with an earnestness more customary to people three times their age. He graciously listened to them. They told him what had happened in their home and asked him if he thought their mother, sisters and brothers had died of the White Plague.

"Very likely they did," he answered. "It could hardly have been any other disease."

If the mother and father had known what the children learned that evening, they might have protected themselves. If they had burned the clothing of the homeless woman; if they had scoured and aired the cabin and had not used the old bedding, they might have lived. The lecturer said he could not say for sure, but he believed that none of their dear ones would have become sick if they had known how to guard against infection.

Osa and Mats hesitated before asking him the next question. It was not true, then, that the gypsy had sent the sickness because they had befriended the one with whom she was angry. It wasn't something special that had happened to them alone. The lecturer assured them that no person had the power to bring sickness upon others that way.

The children thanked him and went to their room. They talked until late that night. The next day they gave notice that they could not tend geese another year, but must leave.

Where were they going? Why, to try to find their father! They must tell him that their mother and the other children had died of a common sickness and not a gypsy's curse. They were glad to have learned the truth. Now it was their responsibility to tell their father.

Osa and Mats set out for their old home on the heath. When they arrived, they were shocked to find the little cabin in flames. They went to the church parsonage, and there they learned that a railroad workman had seen their father at Malmberget, far up in Lapland. He had been working in a mine and might still be there.

When the clergyman heard that the children wanted to go in search of their father, he took out a map and showed them how far it was to Malmberget. Then he tried to convince them not to make the difficult journey. The children insisted that they must find their father; he had left home believing something that was not true, and they must tell him that it was all a misunderstanding.

Osa and Mats did not want to spend their little savings by purchasing railway tickets. They decided, instead, to hike to Malmberget. It was one decision they never regretted, because the trip proved to be remarkably beautiful.

Before they were out of Småland, they stopped at a farmhouse to buy food. The housewife was a kind, motherly soul who took an interest in the children. She asked them who they were and where they came from, and they told her their story.

"Dear, dear! Dear, dear!" she said time and again as they talked. Then she patted them on the head and stuffed them with all kinds of goodies, for which she would not accept a cent. When they were ready to leave, the woman asked them to stop at her brother's farm in the next township. Of course the children were delighted.

"Give him my greetings and tell him what has happened to you," said the peasant woman.

This the children did and were well treated. At every farm after that it was always "If you happen to go in such and such a direction, stop there or there and tell them what has happened to you."

At every farmhouse to which they were sent, there was always a consumptive. So as Osa and Mats went through the country, they taught the people how to combat that dreadful disease—the White Plague, which was sometimes called consumption, or tuberculosis.

Long, long before that, back when the Black Plague was ravaging the country, it was said that another boy and a girl were seen wandering from house to house. The boy carried a rake, and if he stopped and raked in front of a house, it meant that many in that house would die, but not all, because the rake had coarse teeth and did not take everything with it. The girl carried a broom, and if she swept a doorstep, it meant that all who lived within must die; the broom made a clean sweep.

It seems strange that in our time two children would wander through the land because of a cruel sickness. These children, however, did not frighten people with a rake and a broom. Osa and Mats said, "We won't just rake the yard and sweep the floors of the house. No, we'll use mop and brush, water and soap. Everything must be clean—inside and outside of the house—and we ourselves will be clean in mind and body. This is the only way to conquer tuberculosis."

One day while still in Lapland, Akka took the boy to Malmberget, where they found little Mats lying unconscious at the mouth of a mining pit. He and Osa had arrived there a short time before. Only that morning he had been roaming around, hoping to see his father. He had ventured too near the shaft and been seriously injured by flying rocks after a dynamite blast.

Thumbietot ran to the edge of the shaft and shouted down to the miners that a boy was hurt. Several came rushing up to little Mats, and two of them carried him to the hut where he and Osa were staying. They did all they could to save him, but it was too late.

Thumbietot felt awfully sorry for Osa. He wanted to help and comfort her, but he knew that if he were to go to her now in the form of a tomten, he would only frighten her.

The night after little Mats was buried, Osa shut herself up in the hut. She sat alone, remembering things her brother had said and done. There was so much to think about that she did not go straight to bed, but sat up most of the night. The more she thought of her brother, the more she realized how hard it would be to live without him. At last she leaned on the table and wept.

"What shall I do now that little Mats is gone?" she sobbed.

It was far along toward morning and Osa, exhausted after the strain of the day, fell asleep. She dreamed that little Mats softly opened the door and entered the room.

"Osa, go and find Father," he said.

"How can I when I don't even know where he is?" she replied in her dream.

"Don't worry," said her brother cheerfully. "I'll send someone to help you."

Just as Osa dreamed that little Mats had said this, there was a knock at the door. It was a real knock, not something she heard in the dream, but she could hardly tell the real from the unreal. As she went to open the door, she thought, "This must be the person little Mats promised to send me."

She was right, too, because it was Thumbietot, who had come to talk with her about her father. When he saw that she was not afraid of him, the tiny boy told her where her father was and how to reach him.

While he was talking, Osa became wide awake. Then she was so terrified at the thought of talking to a tomten that she could not say thank you or anything else. She slammed the door.

When she did that, she thought she saw an expression of pain flash across the little tomten's face, but she couldn't help what she did. She was beside her-self with fright. She jumped into bed and pulled the covers over her head.

Still...she had a feeling that he meant well by her, so the next day she did exactly what he had told her to do.

Chapter Fifteen

With the Laplanders

One afternoon in July, it rained frightfully up around Lake Luossajaure. The Laplanders, who lived mostly in the open during the summer, had crawled under a big tent and were squatting round the fire, drinking coffee.

The new settlers on the eastern shore of the lake worked diligently to have their homes ready before the severe Arctic winter set in. They were puzzled by the Laplanders, who, although they had lived in the far north for centuries, had never thought they needed any better protection than a tent.

The Laplanders could not understand the new settlers, either—why they put so much effort into getting ready for winter, when they only needed a few reindeer and a tent. Laplanders simply drove poles into the ground, spread covers over them, and their abodes were ready. They didn't have to think about decorating or furnishings. The principal thing was to scatter spruce twigs on the floor, lay out a few skins, and hang up the kettle for cooking reindeer meat.

While the Laplanders were chatting over their coffee cups, a rowboat coming from the Kiruna side pulled ashore at the Lapps' quarters. A man accompanied by a girl between thirteen and fourteen years of age got out of the boat. The girl was Osa.

Dogs barked a noisy welcome and bounded down to the

newcomers, and a man poked his head out of the tent opening to see what was going on. He was glad to see the workman; he was a friend of the Laplanders—a generous and sociable man who spoke their native language.

"You're just in time, Söderberg," the Laplander said. "The coffee pot is on the fire. No one can do any work in the rain, so come in and tell us the news."

Amid a great deal of laughter and joking, places were made for Söderberg and Osa, even though the tent was already crowded with people. Osa couldn't understand Lappish, so she simply looked in wonderment at the kettle and coffee pot, the fire and smoke, the Lapp men and women, the children and dogs, the walls and floor, the coffee cups and tobacco pipes, and the multi-colored costumes and crude implements. All this was new to her.

Suddenly she lowered her glance, conscious that everyone in the tent was looking at her. Söderberg must have said something about her because the men and women took the short pipes from their mouths and stared at her in open-eyed awe. The Laplander at her side patted her shoulder and nodded, saying in Swedish, "Bra, bra!" (Good, good!). A Lapp woman filled a cup with coffee and passed it, while a Lapp boy, who was about Osa's own age, wriggled and crawled between the squatters to be near her. Osa sensed that Söderberg was telling the Laplanders that her little brother, Mats, had just passed away. She wished he would ask about her father instead.

The tomten had said that he lived with the Lapps camping west of Lake Luossajaure, and she had begged permission to ride up on a sand truck to look for him since no regular passenger trains went that far. Both laborers and foremen had assisted her, and an engineer had sent Söderberg across the lake with her because he spoke the Lapp language. She had hoped to meet her father as soon as she arrived. Her glance wandered anxiously from face to face, but her father was not there.

She noticed that the Lapps and the Swede, Söderberg, grew more and more solemn as they talked among themselves. The Lapps shook their heads and tapped their foreheads, as if they were speaking of someone who was not quite right in his mind.

She could no longer endure the suspense and asked Söderberg what the Laplanders knew of her father.

"They say he has gone fishing," said the man, "and they're not sure he can get back to the camp tonight. When the weather clears, one of them will go in search of him."

He turned to the Lapps, and they continued their conversation. He didn't want to give Osa an opportunity to question him further about Jon Esserson.

The Next Morning

Ola Serka himself, who was the most distinguished man in the Lapp community, had said that he would find Osa's father, but he was in no hurry. He sat outside the tent, thinking about Jon Esserson and wondering how to tell him of his daughter's arrival. It would require diplomacy in order for Jon Esserson not to become alarmed and flee. He was an odd sort of man who was afraid of children. He used to say that the sight of them made him so sad that he couldn't endure it.

While Ola Serka deliberated, Osa and Aslak, the young Lapp boy who had stared so hard at her the night before, sat on the ground in front of the tent and talked. Aslak had been to school and could speak Swedish. He was telling Osa about the life of the Samefolk, assuring her that they fared better than other people. Osa thought they lived wretchedly, and she told him so.

"You don't know what you are talking about," said Aslak. "Stay with us for a week, and you will find that we are the happiest people on earth."

"If I stayed a whole week, I'd be choked by the tent smoke," Osa retorted.

"Don't say that," protested the boy. "You don't know anything about us. Here—I'll tell you a story that will help you understand that the longer you stay with us, the happier you will be. Please listen."

Aslak began to tell Osa about the Black Plague. He wasn't

sure if it had gone through the real Sameland—where he and Osa now were—but in Jämtland it had raged so brutally among the Samefolk, who lived in the forests and mountains there, that all had died except a boy of fifteen. Among the Swedes, too, who lived in the valleys, only one was left—a fifteen-year-old girl.

The Lapp boy and the Swedish girl separately walked through the desolate country in search of other human beings. Toward spring they happened upon each other.

Aslak continued: "The girl asked the boy to accompany her south, where she might find some Swedish people.

"'I'll take you wherever you wish to go,' said the boy, 'but not before winter. Now that it's spring, my reindeer must go west to the mountains. You know that we of the Samefolk must follow our reindeer.'

"The Swedish girl was the daughter of wealthy parents. She was accustomed to living under a roof, sleeping in a bed and eating at a table. She had always thought that the mountaineers, who lived under the open sky, were unfortunate people...but she was afraid to go home.

"'At least let me go with you to the mountains,' she said to the boy, 'so that I won't have to be alone and never hear the sound of a human voice.'

"The boy welcomed her company, so the girl followed him and his reindeer to the mountains. The herd looked forward to the good pastures there and traveled long distances every day.

There was no time to pitch tents. The two teenagers had to lie on the snowy ground and sleep when the reindeer stopped to graze. The girl often sighed and complained of being so tired that she must return to the valley. Nevertheless, she went along because she was afraid of being left without companionship.

"When they reached the highlands, the boy pitched a tent for the girl on a pretty hill that sloped toward a mountain brook. In the evening he lassoed and milked the reindeer, and gave the girl milk to drink. He offered her dried reindeer meat and reindeer cheese, which his people had stowed away on the mountain heights when they were there the summer before.

"Still the girl complained. She would eat neither reindeer meat nor reindeer cheese, nor would she drink reindeer milk. She could not get used to squatting in the tent nor to lying on the ground with a reindeer skin and spruce twigs for a bed. The son of the mountains only smiled, and he continued to treat her kindly.

"After a few days, the girl went up to him when he was milking and asked if she could help him. Then she started the fire under the kettle in which the reindeer meat was to be cooked. She also took on the tasks of carrying water and making cheese.

Time passed pleasantly. The weather was mild, and food was easy to get. Together the girl and boy set snares for game, fished for salmon in the rapids and picked cloudberries in the marsh.

"At summer's end, they moved down the mountains and pitched their tent where the pine and leaf forests met. They worked hard every day, but fared even better, for food was even more plentiful than in the summer because of the game. When the snow came and the lakes began to freeze, they moved east toward the pine forests.

"As soon as the tent was up, the winter's work began. The boy taught the girl how to make twine from reindeer sinews, to treat skins, to make shoes and clothing from hides, to make combs and tools from reindeer horn, to travel on skis, and to drive a sled drawn by reindeer.

"After they had lived through the dark winter and the sun began to shine all day and most of the night, the boy said to the girl that now he would accompany her south so that she could find some of her own people. The girl looked at him, astonished.

"'Why do you want to send me away? Would you rather be alone with your reindeer?'

"'I thought you were the one who wanted to get away,' said the boy.

"'I have lived the life of the Samefolk for almost a year now,' replied the girl. 'I can't return to my people and live their shut-in life after wandering freely on mountains and in forests. Don't send me away. Let me stay with you. Your way of living is better than ours.'

"She stayed with him for the rest of her life and never again longed for the valleys. You too, Osa— If you were to stay with us for a month, you would never want to leave us."

So Aslak, the Lapp boy, finished his story.

His father, Ola Serka, took the pipe from his mouth and stood up. He understood more Swedish than he was willing to let anyone know, and he had overheard his son's story. While he was listening, it had suddenly come to him how to handle this delicate matter of telling Jon Esserson that his daughter had come in search of him.

Ola Serka went down to Lake Luossajaure and walked along the strand until he saw a man sitting on a rock, fishing. The fisherman was gray-haired and bent. His eyes blinked wearily, and there was something helpless about him. He looked like a man who had tried to carry a burden too heavy for him, or to solve a problem too difficult for him.

"You must have had good luck with your fishing, Jon, since you've been at it all night," said the mountaineer in his native language.

The fisherman gave a start, then looked up. The bait on his hook was gone, and not one fish lay on the strand beside him. He quickly baited the hook and tossed the line out over the water. Meanwhile, the mountaineer squatted on the grass beside him.

"I'd like your opinion, Jon," said Ola. "You know that my little daughter died last winter, and we've missed her."

"Yes, I know," said the fisherman with a frown...as though he hated being reminded of the death of a child.

"It's not worthwhile to spend one's life grieving," said the Laplander.

"I suppose it isn't."

"I'm thinking of adopting another child, Jon. Don't you think it would be a good idea?"

"That depends on the child, Ola."

"I'll tell you what I know of the girl," said his friend. Then he told the fisherman that around midsummer-time, two children—a boy and a girl—had come to the mines to look for their father. Since their father was away, they had stayed to wait for him. While there, the boy had been killed. Ola gave a clear description of how brave the girl had been and of how she had won the admiration and sympathy of everyone. She was a very special little girl.

"Is she the girl you want to adopt?" asked the fisherman.

"Yes," replied the Lapp. "When we heard her story, we were all sympathetic and commented among ourselves that such a good sister would also make a good daughter, and we hoped that she would come to live with us."

The fisherman sat thinking. It was obvious that he continued the conversation only to please his friend.

"I presume the girl is one of your people."

"No," said Ola, "she doesn't belong to the Samefolk."

"Then perhaps she's the daughter of some new settler and is accustomed to the life here."

"No, she is from the far south," replied Ola, as if this were of little importance.

The fisherman grew more interested.

"Don't adopt her, Ola. I doubt that she could stand living in a tent in the winter, since she was not brought up that way."

"She will find kind parents and brothers and sisters in our tent," insisted Ola Serka. "It's worse to be alone than to feel the cold."

The fisherman became more and more anxious to prevent the adoption. It seemed as if he could not bear the thought of a child of Swedish parents being taken in by Laplanders.

"You just said that she had a father working at the mine."

"He's dead," said the Lapp.

"Have you investigated the matter, Ola?"

"Why should I?" replied the Lapp. "Would the girl and her brother have had to roam the country if their father were living? Would two children have been forced to care for themselves if they had a father? The girl believes he's alive, but he must be dead."

The man with the tired eyes turned to Ola.

"What is the girl's name, Ola?"

The mountaineer thought awhile, then said, "I don't remember. I'll ask her."

"Ask her! Is she already here?"

"She's at the camp."

"Ola! Have you taken her in before knowing her father's wishes?"

"What do I care about her father's wishes? Even if he isn't dead, he doesn't care."

The fisherman threw his rod to the ground and stood up with an abruptness that startled the Laplander.

"If her father is living, he must be haunted by memories and can't keep a steady job," the mountaineer continued. "What kind of a father would that be for a girl?"

While Ola was still talking, the fisherman started up the strand.

"Where are you going, Jon?"

"I want to see your foster daughter, Ola."

"Good," said the Lapp. "I think you'll agree that she will be a good daughter to me."

The Swede walked so fast that the Laplander could hardly keep up with him.

After a moment, Ola said, "Oh, now I recall her name; it's Osa."

Jon walked even faster, and his friend could have laughed aloud.

When they were within sight of the tents, Ola explained, "She came to us Samefolk to find her father—not to become my foster child. But if she doesn't find him, I'll be glad to adopt her."

The fisherman broke into a run, and Ola chuckled.

When the man from Kiruna, who had brought Osa to the tent, went home later in the day, he had two people with him in the boat. They sat close together, holding hands as if they never wanted to part.

The two people were Jon Esserson and his daughter. Jon looked less bent-over and weary, and his eyes were clearer, as if he had found the answer to a troublesome question. And Osa no longer glanced longingly about, for she had found her father, and now she could be a child again.

Chapter Sixteen

Homeward Bound

The First Day of Travel

The boy sat on the goosey-gander's back and rode high among the clouds. Some thirty geese, in regular order, flew rapidly southward. There was a rustling of feathers, and the many wings beat the air so noisily that Nils could scarcely hear his own voice. Akka from Kebnekaise flew in the lead. After her came Yksi and Kaksi, Kolme and Naljä, Viisi and Kuusi, Morton Goosey-Gander and Dunfin. The six goslings which had accompanied the flock the autumn before had left to look after themselves. Instead, the adult geese were taking twenty-two goslings that had grown up in the glen that summer. Eleven flew to the right, eleven to the left, and they did their best to fly at even distances like the adult birds.

This was the first time that the young ones had been on a long trip, and at first they found it hard to keep up with the rapid flight.

"Akka from Kebnekaise! Akka from Kebnekaise!" they cried plaintively.

"What's the matter?" the leader goose answered.

"Our wings are tired of moving, our wings are tired of moving!" wailed the goslings.

"The longer you keep it up, the better it will go," replied the leader goose without slowing. She was quite right, too, for when the goslings had flown two hours longer, they no longer complained of being tired.

Soon they were hungry. In the mountain glen they had been accustomed to eating all day long.

"Akka, Akka, Akka from Kebnekaise!" wailed the goslings pitifully.

"What's the matter now?" asked the leader goose.

"We're so hungry, we can't fly anymore!" whimpered the goslings. "We're so hungry, we can't fly anymore!"

"Wild geese must learn to eat air and drink wind," answered the leader goose, and she kept right on flying.

It actually seemed as if the young ones were learning to live on wind and air, for when they had flown a little longer, they said nothing more about being hungry.

The goose flock was still in the mountain regions, and the adult geese called out the names of the peaks as they flew past, so that the goslings could learn them. After they had been calling out for some time, "This is Portsojåkkå, this is Sarektjåkkå, this is Sulitjelma," and so on, the goslings became impatient again.

"Akka, Akka, Akka!" they screamed.

"What's wrong?" snapped the leader goose.

"We haven't room in our heads for any more awful names!" shrieked the goslings.

"The more you put into your heads, the more you can get into them," returned the leader goose, and she continued to call out the odd names.

The boy sat thinking that it was about time the wild geese turned south, for so much snow had fallen that the ground was white as far as he could see. There was no use denying that life in the glen had become disagreeable. Rain and fog had succeeded each other without any relief, and even if it did clear up once in a while, frost would set in. Berries and mushrooms upon which the boy had subsisted during the summer were either frozen or

decayed. Finally he had been compelled to eat raw fish—something he disliked. The days had grown short, and the long evenings and late mornings were boring for one who could not sleep the whole time that the sun was away.

Now, at last, the goslings' wings had grown and the geese were on their way south. The boy was so happy that he laughed and sang as he rode on the goose's back. It was not only because of the darkness and cold that he longed to get away from Lapland.

The first weeks there the boy had not been the least bit homesick. He thought he'd never seen such magnificent country. All he had to worry about were mosquitoes.

The boy had seen very little of the goosey-gander because the big white gander thought only of his Dunfin and was unwilling to leave her even for a moment. So Thumbietot had stayed with Akka and Gorgo, and the three of them passed many happy hours together.

The two birds had taken him with them on long trips. He had stood on snowcapped Mount Kebnekaise, had looked down at the glaciers and visited high cliffs seldom climbed by humans. Akka had shown him hidden mountain dales and let him peek into caves where mother wolves brought up their young. He had also become acquainted with tame reindeer grazing in herds along the shores of beautiful Torne Lake, and he had been down to the magnificent falls and brought greetings to the bears from their friends and relatives in Västmanland.

He had seen and done wonderful things, yet ever since he had seen Osa, he wished for the day when he might go home with Morton Goosey-Gander and be a normal human being once more. He wanted to be himself again so that Osa would no longer be afraid to talk to him and would not shut the door in his face.

Now they were speeding south. The boy waved his cap and cheered when he saw the first pine forest. He greeted the first gray cabin, the first goat, the first cat, the first chicken.

They were continually meeting birds of passage, flying in even larger flocks than when he saw them last spring.

"Where are you bound, wild geese?" called the passing birds. "Where are you bound?"

"Like you, we're going abroad," answered the geese.

"Your goslings aren't ready to fly," screamed the others. "They'll never cross the sea with those weak wings!"

The Laplanders and their reindeer were also leaving the mountains. When the wild geese sighted the reindeer, they circled down and called out, "We've enjoyed your company!"

"A pleasant journey to you and a welcome back next summer!" bellowed the reindeer.

When bears saw the wild geese, however, they pointed them out to their cubs and growled, "Look at those geese. They're so afraid of a little cold, they don't dare stay home over the winter."

The parent geese were ready with a retort and cried to their goslings, "Look at those lazy animals! They stay at home and sleep half the year rather than going to the effort of traveling south!"

Down in the pine forest, young grouse huddled together and looked longingly after the merry bird flocks flying south. "When will our turn come?" they asked the mother grouse.

"You will just have to stay at home with Mama and Papa," she said.

THE TRAVELS OF

BOOK TWO

NILS HOLGERSSON

Chapter Seventeen

Legends From Härjedalen

Tuesday, October fourth.

After three days of travel through rain and fog, the boy longed for a sheltered nook to rest awhile. At last the geese stopped to feed and ease their wings. To his relief, Nils saw an observation tower on a hill close by and dragged himself to it. When he had climbed to the top of the tower, he found a party of tourists there. He quickly crept into a dark corner and went to sleep.

When he awoke, he began to feel uneasy because the tourists were lingering so long in the tower, telling stories. He thought they would never leave. Morton Goosey-Gander couldn't come for him while they were there, and he knew, of course, that the wild geese were in a hurry to continue the journey. In the middle of a story he thought he heard honking and the beating of wings, as if the geese were flying away, but he didn't dare to venture over to the balustrade to find out if it was so.

When the tourists were gone and the boy could crawl from his hiding place, he didn't see the wild geese and Morton Goosey-Gander hadn't come to get him. He called, "Here am I, where are you?" but his traveling companions did not appear.

While he was wondering what to do, Bataki, the raven, flew up beside him.

The boy welcomed him: "Bataki, I'm glad you're here! Do you know where Morton Goosey-Gander and the wild geese are?"

"I've just come with a message from them," replied the raven. "Akka saw a hunter prowling on the mountain and didn't dare to wait for you. She and the flock went on ahead. Get on my back and you'll soon be with your friends."

The boy quickly got on.

Bataki would have caught up with the geese if he hadn't been hindered by fog. It was as if the morning sun had awakened it to life. Light veils of mist rose suddenly from the lake, from fields and from the forest. They thickened and spread, and soon the entire ground was hidden from sight by white, rolling fog.

Bataki flew above it in clear air and sparkling sunshine, but the wild geese must have circled down among the damp clouds. The boy and the raven called and called, but got no response.

"This is bad luck," said Bataki. "At least we know they're traveling south, and of course I'll find them as soon as the fog clears."

The boy was distressed at the thought of being parted from Morton Goosey-Gander now when the geese were on the wing and the big white one might come upon all sorts of problems. After Thumbietot had been worrying for two hours or more, he remarked to himself that so far there hadn't been a serious accident.

Just then he heard a rooster crowing. The boy leaned forward on the raven's back and shouted, "What's the name of the country I'm traveling over?"

"It's called Härjedalen, Härjedalen, Härjedalen," crowed the rooster.

"How does it look down there where you are?" the boy asked.

"Cliffs in the west, woods in the east, broad valleys across the whole country," replied the rooster.

"Thank you," shouted the boy.

When they had gone a little farther, he heard a crow cawing down in the fog.

"What kind of people live in this country?" shouted the boy.

"Good, thrifty peasants," answered the crow. "Good, thrifty peasants."

"Thanks," replied the boy.

Farther on, he heard singing and yodeling.

"Is there a large city in this part of the country?" the boy called.

"What—what—who's there? Who are you?" faltered the human voice.

"Is there a large city in this region?" the boy repeated.

"Tell me who you are!" the person shouted back.

"I might have known I couldn't get any information when I asked a human being a civil question," the boy retorted.

The fog went away as suddenly as it had come. Then the boy saw a beautiful landscape with high cliffs as in Jämtland, but there were no large, flourishing settlements on the mountain slopes. The villages lay far apart, and the farms were small. Bataki and Nils followed the stream south until they came within sight of a village. There the raven alighted in a stubble field and let the boy dismount.

"In the summer, grain grew on this ground," said Bataki. "See if you can find something edible.

The boy went to look and soon found a blade of wheat. As he picked out the grains and ate them, he listened to Bataki.

"Do you see that mountain?" Bataki asked.

"Mhm. What about it?" asked the boy.

"It is called Sånfjället," continued the raven. "Wolves were plentiful there once upon a time."

"It seems like an ideal place for wolves," the boy said.

"The people who lived here in the valley were often attacked by them," remarked the raven.

"If you know a good wolf story, I'd like to hear it," said the boy.

"Well, a long, long time ago" Bataki began, "the wolves

from Sånfjället ambushed a traveling salesman. The man was from Hede, a village a few miles down the valley. It was winter-time, and the wolves made for him as he was driving over the ice on Lake Ljusna. There were about nine or ten, and the man from Hede had an old horse, so there was little hope of his escaping.

"When the man heard the wolves howl and saw how many were after him, he lost his head. It didn't occur to him to dump his casks and jugs out of the sled to lighten the load. He only whipped up the horse, and the wolves gained on him. The shores were deserted, and he was fourteen miles from the nearest farm. He thought his final hour had come.

"While he sat there, terrified, he saw something move in the brush that had been set in the ice to mark the road. When he discovered who was walking there, his fear grew even more intense.

"Between him and the wolves was an old woman named Finn-Malin, who roamed the highways and byways. She was a hunchback and slightly lame, so he recognized her from a dis-tance.

"The sled had hidden the wolves from her view, and the man knew that if he were to drive on without warning her, she would walk right into their jaws. While they attacked her, he could get away.

"Finn-Malin walked slowly, bent over a cane. She would be doomed if he didn't help her. Even if he were to stop and take

her into the sled, more than likely the wolves would catch up
with them, and he and she and the horse would all be killed.
Wouldn't it be better to sacrifice one life—hers? Would her
death bother him afterward? What if people found out that he
had abandoned her? Oh, it was a terrible temptation!

"'I wish I hadn't seen her,'" he muttered.

"The wolves howled savagely. The horse reared, plunged
forward and dashed past the beggar woman. She had heard the
howling of the wolves. As the man from Hede drove by, he saw
that the old woman knew what was coming. She stood motionless, her mouth open to cry, her arms stretched out for help, but
she neither cried nor tried to throw herself into the sled.
Something seemed to have turned her to stone.

"'It was I,' thought the man. 'I must have looked like a
demon as I passed.'

"He tried to feel satisfied, now that he was sure of escape,
but his heart reproached him. This horrible act of inhumanity
would ruin his life, and he knew it.

"'Come what may,' he said, reining in the horse, 'I can't
leave her to the wolves!'

"It was hard to turn the horse, but he managed it and drove
back to her.

"'Quick! Get in!' he shouted. "You might stay home once
in awhile, you old hag. My horse and I will come to grief because
of you."

"Finn-Malin didn't reply.

"'The horse has already gone thirty-five miles today, and
the load hasn't lightened since you got on it.'

"The sled runners crunched on the ice, but the man heard
the wolves panting and knew they were almost upon him. 'We're
done for!' he said. 'Much good it was to attempt to save you,
Finn-Malin.'

"Until this point the old woman had kept silent—like one
who is accustomed to abuse—but now she said, 'Why didn't you
throw your wares overboard and lighten the load? You could
return tomorrow and pick them up.'

"Surprised that he hadn't thought of it himself, the man

tossed the reins to Finn-Malin, loosened the ropes that bound the casks and pitched them out. The wolves stopped to see what he had thrown out, and the sled moved ahead of them.

"'If the wolves catch up, I'll give myself up to them so you can escape,' Finn-Malin said.

"The man tried to push a heavy brewer's vat from the long sled. Then he paused as if he wasn't sure that he wanted to throw it out. Actually he was thinking, 'It's only my stupidity that keeps me from thinking of a solution to this dilemma.'

"Suddenly he laughed, and Finn-Malin became alarmed, thinking he had gone mad, but the man from Hede was only laughing at himself.

"'Listen!' he said. 'Thanks for offering to throw yourself to the wolves, but you won't have to do that. No matter what I do, you just drive to Linsäll. Wake the townspeople and tell them that I'm alone on the ice, surrounded by wolves. Ask them to come and help me.'

"The man waited until the wolves had almost caught up with the sled. Then he rolled the big brewer's vat onto the ice, jumped down and crawled in under it. It was a huge vat, large enough to hold a whole Christmas brew. The wolves pounced on it and bit at the hoops, but the vat was too heavy for them to move and they couldn't get at the man inside.

"He knew he was safe and scoffed at the wolves. After awhile he was serious again. 'Next time I get into trouble,' he thought, 'I'll remember this vat and bear in mind that there's never a reason to harm myself or others. There is always a third way out if only I can hit upon it.'"

Bataki had finished his narrative. The boy knew that the raven never spoke unless there was some special meaning behind his words. He asked, "Why did you tell me that story?"

"I thought of it when I looked at Sånfjället," replied the raven.

Now they had traveled farther down Lake Ljusna, and in an hour or so they reached Kolsätter, close to the border of Hälsingland. The raven alighted near a little hut that had no windows—only a shutter. From the chimney rose sparks and smoke, and from inside came the sound of hammering.

"Every time I see this smithy," observed the raven, "I'm
reminded that there used to be such skilled blacksmiths here in
Härjedalen, and especially in this village, that there weren't any
better in the whole country."

"Well, Bataki, do you have a story to tell me about them?"
the boy asked.

"Yes," replied the raven. "I remember one about a smith
from Härjedalen who once invited two other master blacksmiths—one from Dalecarlia and one from Värmland—to compete with him at nail making. The challenge was accepted, and
the three blacksmiths met here at Kolsätter. The Dalecarlian
began. He forged a dozen nails so even and smooth and sharp
that they couldn't be improved upon. After him came the
Värmlander. He, too, forged a dozen nails which were quite perfect. Besides that, he finished them in half the time that it took
the Dalecarlian. When the judges saw this, they told the
Härjedal smith that it wouldn't be worth his trying since he
couldn't possibly forge better than the Dalecarlian or faster than
the Värmlander.

"'There must be another way of excelling,' insisted the
Härjedal smith. He placed the iron on the anvil without heating
it at the forge. He hammered it hot and forged nail after nail
without the use of anvil or bellows. None of the judges had ever
seen a blacksmith wield a hammer more masterfully, and the
Härjedal smith was proclaimed the best in the land."

With these words, Bataki was silent, and the boy grew even
more thoughtful. "Why did you tell me that story, Bataki?" he
asked.

"It just popped into my mind when I saw the old smithy
again," said the raven.

The two travelers rose into the air, and the raven carried
the boy south till they reached Lillhärdal Parish, where he alighted on a leafy mound at the top of a ridge.

"Do you know where you are now?" asked the raven.

"No."

"You are standing on a grave," said Bataki. "Beneath this

mound lies the first settler in Härjedalen. He was an innovative fellow, that one."

"You must have a story about him, too," said the boy.

"I haven't heard much about him, but I think he was a Norwegian. He had been in the service of a Norwegian king but got into disfavor and had to flee the country.

"Then he entered the service of the Swedish king, who lived at Uppsala. After awhile he asked for the hand of the king's sister in marriage. When the king wouldn't give him such a high-born bride, he eloped with her. By that time he had gotten into such disfavor that it wasn't safe for him to live either in Sweden or Norway, and he didn't want to move to a foreign country.

"'There must be a way out of this predicament,' he thought. With his servants and his treasures, he journeyed through Dalecarlia until he reached the desolate forests beyond the outskirts of the province. There he built houses and tilled the land. So, you see, he was the first man to settle in this part of the country."

As the boy listened to the last story, he looked very serious. "Why have you told me this?" he repeated.

Bataki twisted and turned and screwed up his eyes, and it was some time before he answered the boy. "Since we are here alone," he said, "let me ask you a question. Have you thought about the tomten's terms that had to be met before you could become a human being again?"

"The only stipulation I've heard about was that I should take the white goosey-gander up to Lapland and bring him back to Skåne safe and sound."

"I thought so," said Bataki, "because when we last met you said there was nothing more contemptible than deceiving a friend. You'd better ask Akka about the terms.

"Did you know she was at your home and talked with the tomten?"

"Akka hasn't told me about it."

"She must have thought it best for you not to know what he said. Naturally she would rather help you than Morton Goosey-Gander."

"It's odd, Bataki. You always have a way of making me worried," said the boy.

"Maybe so," continued the raven, "but this time I think you will be grateful for my information. The tomten said you would become a normal human being again if you returned Morton Goosey-Gander so your mother could lay him on the block and chop his head off."

The boy jumped up. "You're lying!"

"Ask Akka yourself," said Bataki. "I see her coming with her flock. Don't forget what I have told you today. There's usually a way out of a difficulty. I'll be interested to hear how you handle this one."

Chapter Eighteen

Värmland and Dalsland

Wednesday, October fifth.

Nils took advantage of a rest period, while Akka was feeding apart from the other wild geese, to ask her if what Bataki had told him was true. Akka couldn't deny it.

Immediately the boy made her promise not to tell the secret to Morton Goosey-Gander. The big white gander was so brave and generous that he might do something rash if he found out what the tomten actually said.

Later the boy sat on the goosey-gander's back, sad and quiet. He heard the wild geese honking to the goslings that now they were in Dalarna and they could see Mount Städjan in the north...now they were flying over Österdal River to Horrmund Lake...now they were coming to Västerdal River. The boy wasn't interested.

"I will probably travel with the wild geese the rest of my life," he said, "and am likely to see more of this land than I care to."

He was still indifferent when the wild geese called out that they had arrived in Värmland and that the stream they were following south was Klarälven.

"I've seen so many rivers already," said the boy, "why should I look at one more?"

All of northern Värmland was composed of vast mountainous tracts through which Klarälven wound, narrow and full of rapids. Here and there was a charcoal kiln, a forest clearing or a few low, chimneyless huts occupied by Finns. The forest as a whole was so large that one might imagine it was far up in Lapland.

A Little Homestead

Thursday, October sixth.

The wild geese followed Klarälven to the big iron foundries at Munkfors. Then they went west to Fryksdalen. Before they got to Lake Fryken, the sky began to grow dusky. They alighted in a little, wet slough on a wooded hill. This was a good refuge for the wild geese, but the boy thought it dismal and wished for a better place to sleep. While he was still high in the air, he had noticed that below the ridge lay a number of farms. When he was on the ground, he went to look for them.

They were farther away than he had thought, and several times he was tempted to turn back. Finally the woods thinned, and he found a road skirting the edge of the trees. From it branched a pretty, birch-bordered lane that led to a farm. He hurried down the lane.

The boy entered a farmyard as large as a city marketplace and enclosed by a long row of red houses. As he crossed the yard, he saw another farm, where the dwelling house faced a gravel path and a wide lawn. Behind the house was a garden. The dwelling itself was small and humble, but the garden was edged by a row of tall mountain ash trees so close together that they formed a wall around it like a high-vaulted chamber, with the lovely blue sky for a ceiling. The mountain ash were thick with clusters of red berries. The grass was still green, of course, but that night there was a full moon, and as the bright moonlight fell upon the grass it looked like silver.

No human being was in sight, and the boy could go wherever he wished. In the garden he saw something that almost cheered him. He had climbed a mountain ash to eat berries, but before he could reach a cluster he caught sight of a barberry bush that was also full of berries. He slid along the ash branch and climbed up into the barberry bush, but he was no sooner there than he discovered a currant bush on which still hung long, red clusters. The garden was full of gooseberries and raspberries and dog rose bushes. There were cabbages and turnips in the vegetable beds...berries on every bush...seeds on the herbs...grain-filled ears on every blade. Of all things, there on the path—no, he could not be mistaken—was a big, red apple that shone in the moonlight.

The boy sat down at the side of the path, with the apple in front of him, and began cutting little pieces from it with his sheath knife. "It wouldn't be so bad to be a tomten if it were always as easy to get good food as it is here," he thought.

He mused as he ate, thinking he might just remain here and let the wild geese travel south without him. "For the life of me, I don't know how I could ever explain to Morton Goosey-Gander that I cannot go home," the boy thought. "It would be better for me to leave him altogether. I could gather enough provisions for the winter—just as well as the squirrels do—and if I lived in a dark corner of the stable or the cowshed, I wouldn't freeze."

Just as he was thinking about this, he heard a light rustle over his head, and a second later something resembling a birch stump stood on the ground beside him. The stump twisted and turned, and two bright dots on top of it glowed like coals of fire. It was a ghostly sort of thing. Then the boy saw that the stump had a hooked beak and big feather circles around its glowing eyes.

"It's a pleasure to meet a living creature," said the boy. "Perhaps you will be kind enough to tell me the name of this place, Mrs. Brown Owl, and what sort of people live here."

That evening, as on all other evenings, the owl had perched on a rung of the big ladder propped against the roof, from which she had looked down toward the gravel walks and grass plots, watching for rats. Very much to her surprise, not a single grayskin had appeared. She saw instead something that looked like a human being, but much, much smaller, moving in the garden.

"That's what's scaring away the rats!" thought the owl. "What can it be? It's not a squirrel, not a kitten, not a weasel. A bird who has lived on an old place like this as long as I have ought to know about everything, but this is beyond my comprehension."

She had been staring at the object that moved on the gravel path until her eyes burned and her curiosity got the better of her. She flew down to the ground to have a closer look at the stranger.

When the boy began to talk, the owl thought, "He has neither claws nor horns," she remarked to herself, "but he may have a poisonous fang or some even more dangerous weapon."

"The place is called Mårbacka," said the owl, "and gentlefolk lived here once upon a time. Who are you?"

"I'm thinking of moving in here," volunteered the boy without answering the owl's question. "Would it be possible, do you think?"

"Oh, yes—but it's not much of a place now compared to what it used to be," said the owl. "You can weather it here, I guess. It all depends upon what you expect to live on. Do you intend to take up the rat chase?"

"No," laughed the boy. "There's more fear of the rats eating me than that I shall do them any harm."

"He can't be as harmless as he says," thought the owl. "All the same, I believe I'll find out." She rose into the air, and in a moment her claws were fastened in Nils Holgersson's shoulder and she was trying to hack his eyes out.

The boy shielded his eyes with one hand and tried to free himself with the other, at the same time screaming for help.

Now I must tell you of a strange coincidence. The very year that Nils Holgersson traveled with the wild geese, there was a woman who thought of writing a book about Sweden. She wanted the book to be suitable for children to read in school. She had thought of this from Christmastime until the following autumn, but not a line of the book had she written. At last she became so tired of the whole thing that she said to herself, "You're just not the person to write the book. Compose stories and legends as usual, and let someone else write this book; it has to be serious and instructive, and it must not contain one untruthful word."

She decided to abandon the book. Still she thought, very naturally, that it would have been pleasant to write something beautiful about Sweden. Then it occurred to her that maybe it was because she lived in a city, with only gray streets and house walls around her, that she couldn't make any headway with the writing. Perhaps if she were to go into the country, where she could see woods and fields, it would go better.

She was from Värmland, and it was perfectly clear to her that she wanted to begin the book with that province. First she would write about the place where she had grown up. It was a little homestead, far removed from the great world, where many old-fashioned customs were retained. She thought that it would be entertaining for children to hear of the many and varied duties which had succeeded one another the year round. She wanted to tell them how her family had celebrated Christmas and New Year and Easter and Midsummer Day…what kind of house furnishings they had...what the kitchen and larder were like...how the cowshed, stable, lodge and bathhouse had looked. But when she wanted to write about it, the pen would not move. Why this was she couldn't in the least understand, but that was what happened every time.

True, she remembered it all as distinctly as if she were still living in the midst of it. She argued with herself that since she was going to the country anyway, maybe she ought to make a little trip to the old homestead so she could see it again before writing about it. She hadn't been there in a very long time, although she had always wanted to be there, no matter in what part of the world she happened to be. She had seen far more pretentious and prettier places, but nowhere could she find such comfort and protection as at the home of her childhood.

It wasn't so easy for her to go home, however. The estate had been sold to people she did not know. She thought they would be kind enough, but she didn't want to talk with strangers. No, she wanted to remember how her home had been when she was a child. That was why she planned to arrive there late in the evening, after the workday was over and the people were indoors.

She had never imagined it would be so wonderful to go home. As she sat in the cart and rode toward the homestead, she fancied that she was growing younger and younger, and that soon she would no longer be an older person with hair that was turning gray, but a little girl in short skirts with a long, golden braid. As she recognized each farm along the road, she dreamed that her father and mother and brothers and sisters would be standing on the porch to welcome her. The old housekeeper would run to the kitchen window to see who was coming, and Nero and Freja and another dog or two would come bounding and jumping up on her.

The nearer she got to the place, the happier she felt. It was autumn, which meant a busy time with a round of duties. It must have been all these duties which prevented her home from ever being humdrum.

Along the way the farmers were digging potatoes, and probably they would be doing the same at her home. That meant

they must begin immediately to grate potatoes and make potato flour. The autumn had been a mild one. She wondered if everything in the garden had already been stored. The cabbages were still out, but maybe the hops had been picked, and all the apples.

They might even be having housecleaning. Autumn fair time was drawing near, and everywhere the cleaning and scouring had to be done before the fair opened. That was regarded as a great event—especially by the servants. It was fun to go into the kitchen on Market Eve and see the newly scoured floor strewn with juniper twigs and the whitewashed walls and the shining copper utensils which were suspended from the ceiling.

Even after the fair festivities were over, there would not be much of a breathing spell because then came the work on the flax. During dog days the flax had been spread out on a meadow to mold. Now it was laid in the old bathhouse, where the stove was lighted to dry it out. When the flax was dry enough to handle, all the women in the neighborhood sat outside the bathhouse and picked the flax to pieces. Then they beat it with swingles (wooden instruments shaped like a large knife) to separate the fine, white fibers from the dry stems. As they worked, the women's hair and clothing were covered with flax seed, but they did not seem to mind it. All day the swingles pounded and the chatter went on, so that when one went near the old bathhouse it sounded as if a blustering storm had broken loose there.

Hardtack baking came after the work with the flax. So did sheep shearing and the servants' moving time. In November there were busy slaughter days, with salting of meats, sausage making, baking of blood pudding and candle steeping. The seamstress who used to sew their homemade dresses had to come at this time, of course, and those were always two pleasant weeks—when the women sat together and busied themselves with sewing. The cobbler, who made shoes for the entire household, sat working at the same time in the menservants' quarters, and one never tired of watching him as he cut the leather and soled and heeled the shoes and put eyelets in the shoestring holes.

The biggest rush came around Christmas. Lucia Day—when the housemaid went around dressed in white, with candles in her hair, and served coffee to everybody at five in the morning—came as a sort of reminder that for the next two weeks they could not count on much sleep. Now they must brew the Christmas ale, steep the Christmas fish in lye, and do the Christmas baking and cleaning.

The dreamer was in the middle of the baking, with pans of Christmas buns and cookie platters all around her, when the driver drew in the reins at the end of the lane as she had requested. She started like one suddenly awakened from a sound sleep. It was depressing for her, who had just imagined herself surrounded by family and friends, to be sitting alone in the late evening. As she climbed from the wagon and walked up the long lane to approach her old home unobserved, she felt so strongly the contrast between now and then that she would have preferred to turn back.

"Why did I come here?" she sighed. "It can't be the way it was when I was little."

Yet she had traveled such a long distance that she might as well do what she had set out to do. She continued to walk on, although she was more depressed with every step that she took.

She had heard that the place had changed, and it certainly had, but she didn't notice. She thought, rather, that everything was quite the same. There was the pond, which used to be full of carp. No one dared fish there because it was her father's wish that the carp be left in peace. Over there were the menservants' quarters, the larder and the barn, with the farmyard bell over one gable and the weather vane over the other. The house yard was like a circular room with no outlook in any direction, as it had been in her father's time. He hadn't the heart to cut down a single bush.

She lingered in the shadow under the big mountain ash at the entrance to the farm and stood looking around. As she stood there, a strange thing happened. A flock of doves came and lit beside her. She could hardly believe that they were real birds, for doves rarely fly after sundown. The moonlight must have awakened them. They must have thought it was dawn and flown from the dovecotes, only to become confused. When they saw a human being, they flew over to her as if she could tell them whether it was day or night.

There had been many flocks of doves at the manor when her parents lived there, for the doves were among the creatures her father had taken as his special responsibility. If one ever mentioned the killing of a dove, it put him in a bad mood. She was pleased that the pretty birds had come to meet her. Had the doves flown out to show her they hadn't forgotten that once upon a time they had a good home there? Perhaps her father had sent his birds with a greeting to her so that she wouldn't feel so sad and lonely when she returned to her former home.

As she thought of this, such an intense longing for the old times welled up within her that her eyes filled with tears. Life had been wonderful in this place.

Weeks of work were broken by many holiday festivities. They had worked hard all day, but in the evening they had gathered around the lamp and read Tegnér and Runeberg, "Fru" Lenngren and "Mamsell" Bremer. They had cultivated grain, but also roses and jasmine. They had spun flax, but had sung folksongs as they spun. They had worked hard at their history and grammar, but they had also played theater and written verses. They had stood at the kitchen stove and prepared food, but had learned, also, to play the flute and guitar, the violin and piano. They had planted cabbages and turnips, peas and beans in one garden, but they had another full of apples and pears and all kinds of berries. They had lived by themselves, and this was why so many stories and legends were stowed away in their memories. They had worn homemade clothes, but they had also been able to lead carefree and independent lives.

"Nowhere else in the world do they know how to get so much out of life as they did at one of these little homesteads in my childhood," she thought. "There was just enough work and just enough play, and every day there was another reason to be happy. I should love to come back here again. Now that I have seen the place, it is hard to leave it."

Half amused, half serious, she turned to the flock of doves and said to them, "Fly to Father and tell him that I long to come home. I have wandered long enough in strange places. Ask him if he can't arrange it so that I may soon return to my childhood home."

The moment she had said this, the flock of doves rose and flew away. She tried to follow them with her eyes, but they vanished. It was as if the whole white company had dissolved in the shimmering air.

The doves had just left when she heard piercing cries from the garden. As she hurried to see what was happening, she saw a tiny tomten struggling with a brown owl. At first she was so astonished that she could not move, but when the tomten cried

again,
she ran to
the fighters
and parted them.
The owl swung up
into a tree.

"Thanks for helping
me," said the tomten, "but
it was stupid of you to let the owl escape. Now how can I get
away? She is sitting up in the tree, watching me."

"I'm sorry. It was thoughtless of me to let the owl go. To
make amends, would you let me accompany you home?" asked
she who wrote stories, surprised that in this unexpected way she
had gotten into a conversation with one of the tiny folk. Still she
wasn't so very surprised. It was as if she had been waiting for
some extraordinary experience while she walked in the moonlight outside her old home.

"The fact is, I had thought of staying here overnight," the
tomten said. "If you would show me a safe sleeping place, I won't
have to return to the forest before daybreak."

"Do I need to show you a place to sleep? Isn't this your
home?"

"You think I'm one of the tiny folk," the boy said, "but I'm a
human being like yourself. I'm only under the spell of a tomten."

"Why, that's remarkable! Would you mind telling me your
story?"

The boy wasn't at all adverse to relating his adventures, and
as the narrative proceeded, his listener grew more and more
astonished and happy.

"What luck to run across someone who has traveled all over Sweden on the back of a goose," thought she. "What he's telling me I will write down in my book. To think that I'd find such help here in my old home—"

Then she remembered. She had sent word to her father by the doves that she longed for home, and almost immediately she had received help with her book. Might this be her father's answer to her prayer?

THE TRAVELS OF
BOOK TWO
NILS HOLGERSSON

Chapter Nineteen
....

The Treasure on the Island

On Their Way to the Sea
....

Friday, October seventh.

From the very start of the autumn trip, the wild geese had flown straight south, but when they left Fryksdalen they turned in another direction, traveling over western Värmland and Dalsland, toward Bohuslän. Oh, that was a memorable trip! By now the goslings were so used to flying that they no longer complained of being tired, and the boy was fast recovering his good humor.

Nils was glad that he had talked with a human being. He felt encouraged when she said that if he continued to do good to everyone he met—as he had been doing—it couldn't possibly be to his disadvantage. She couldn't tell him how to regain his natural size, but she had given him a little hope, and that hope had inspired him to think of a way to prevent the white gander from going home.

While they were flying high in the sky, Nils said to his friend, "You know...we would be awfully bored if we had to stay home all winter after being on a trip like this." As though he'd just thought of it, the boy suggested, "Let's go abroad with the geese."

"What? You don't mean that!" objected the goosey-gander. Since he had proved to the wild geese that he was able to travel with them all the way up to Lapland, he was quite ready to return to the goose pen in Holger Nilsson's cowshed.

The boy gazed down on Värmland, where the birch woods, leafy groves and gardens were clad in red and yellow autumn colors. "I don't think I've ever seen the earth beneath us as lovely as it is today," he said. "The lakes are like blue satin bands. Don't you think it would be a mistake to settle down in West Vemminghög and never see any more of the world?"

"I thought you wanted to go home to your mother and father and show them what a splendid boy you had become," replied the gander. All summer he had been dreaming of the proud moment when he alighted in the yard in front of Holger Nilsson's cabin and showed Dunfin and the six goslings to the geese and chickens, the cows and the cat, and to Mother Holger Nilsson herself. He was not at all pleased with the boy's proposal.

"Don't you think yourself that it would be hard not to travel and never again see Sweden's beauty?"

The goosey-gander sadly relented. "I would rather see the fat grainfields of Söderslätt than these lean hills, but if you really want to continue the trip, I won't leave you."

"That's the answer I expected from you, my loyal friend," said the boy, and his voice betrayed that he was relieved.

Later, when they traveled over Bohuslän, the boy observed that the mountain stretches were more continuous, the valleys were more like little ravines blasted in the rock foundation, and the long lakes at their base were as black as if they had come from the underworld. Oh! this too was magnificent country. As the boy saw it—with now a strip of sun and now a shadow—he thought there was something strange and wild about it. He didn't know why, but the idea came to him that at one time, strong and brave heroes were in these mystical regions, and they had passed through dangerous and daring adventures. The old passion of wanting to share in exciting adventures awoke in him.

"I might miss not being in danger of my life at least once every day or two," he thought. "Anyhow, it's best to be content with things the way they are."

He didn't mention any of this to the white gander, because the geese were now flying over Bohuslän with all the speed they could muster, and the big goosey-gander was puffing so hard that he would not have had the strength to reply.

The sun was far down in the horizon and disappeared every now and then behind a hill. Still the geese kept forging ahead. Finally, in the west, they saw a shining strip of light that grew broader with every wing stroke. Soon the sea spread before them, milk white with a shimmer of rose red and sky blue. When they had circled past the coastal cliffs, they saw the sun again as it hung over the sea—big and red and ready to plunge into the waves.

As the boy gazed at the endless sea and the red evening sun, which had such a gentle, friendly glow that he dared to look directly at it, he felt a sense of peace penetrate his soul.

"There's no sense in being sad, Nils Holgersson," said the sun. "This is a beautiful world to live in. You're free, and you have a magnificent dome of open sky above you."

The Gift of the Wild Geese

....

The geese stood sleeping on a little rock island just beyond Fjällbacka. When it drew on toward midnight and the moon hung high in the heavens, old Akka shook the sleepiness out of her eyes. She walked around and awakened Yksi and Kaksi, Kolme and Neljä, Viisi and Kuusi. Last of all, she gave Thumbietot a nudge with her bill, startling him.

"What...what is it, Mother Akka?" he asked, getting up in alarm.

"Nothing to worry about," said the leader goose soothingly. "We seven who have been together a long time want to fly out to sea tonight, and we wondered if you would like to come along."

The boy knew that Akka would not have invited him

unless she had a good reason, so he promptly seated himself on her back. The flight was straight west. The wild geese first flew over a belt of large and small islands near the coast, then over a broad expanse of open sea, until they reached the cluster known as the Väder Islands. All of the islands were low and rocky, and in the moonlight one could see that they were large.

Akka looked at one of the smallest islands and alighted there. It consisted of a round, gray stone hill with a wide cleft across it into which the sea had cast fine, white sea sand and a few shells.

As the boy slid from the goose's back, he noticed something that looked like a jagged stone. A vulture had chosen the rock island for a night harbor! Before the boy had time to wonder why the geese had recklessly alighted so near a dangerous enemy, the bird flew up to them and the boy recognized Gorgo, the eagle. Evidently Akka and Gorgo had arranged the meeting, for neither of them was taken by surprise.

"Gorgo," said Akka, "I didn't expect you to be at the meeting place ahead of us. Have you been here long?"

"I did come early in the evening to keep my appointment with you," replied the eagle, "but I fear I wasn't successful in carrying out your commission."

"I'm sure you have done more than you care to admit," said Akka, "but before you tell us what happened, I shall ask Thumbietot to help me find something that's supposed to be buried on this island."

The boy stood looking admiringly at two beautiful seashells, but when Akka said his name, he glanced up.

"You must have wondered, Thumbietot, why we altered our course to fly here to the West Sea," said Akka.

"Oh, I did think it was odd," answered the boy, "but I knew that you always have a good reason for what you do."

"You hold a high opinion of me," replied Akka, "but you may lose it now. We have probably made this journey in vain.

"Years ago, two other geese and I encountered terrible storms during a spring flight and were wind-driven to this island. When we discovered that there was only open sea ahead of us, we thought we'd be swept so far out that we could never find our way back to land. To save ourselves, we lay down on the waves between these bare cliffs.

"The storm forced us to remain here for several days, and we began to suffer from hunger. Once we ventured up to the cleft on this island, looking for food. We didn't find any grass, but we saw some bags half buried in the sand. We hoped to find grain in the bags and pulled at them until we tore the cloth. To our dismay, no grain poured out—only shining gold pieces. We didn't have any use for them, of course, so we left them where they were. We haven't thought of the find in all these years, but this autumn something has come up to make us desire gold. We don't know if the treasure is still here, but we've traveled all this way to ask you to help us find it."

With a shell in each hand, the boy jumped down into the cleft and began to scoop up sand. He didn't find any bags, but after the hole he'd dug was good and deep, he heard the clink of metal and knew he'd found a gold piece. Then he dug with his fingers and felt more coins in the sand.

"Mother Akka, the bags have rotted and fallen apart," he shouted, "and the money is scattered in the sand."

"Good, good," said Akka. "Leave the gold there. Fill in the hole and smooth it over so no one will notice that the sand has been disturbed."

The boy did as he was told, but when he left the rock cleft, he was astonished to see that the wild geese were lined up, with Akka in the lead, and were marching toward him with great solemnity.

The geese stopped in front of him, and all bowed their heads many times, looking so grave that he had to take off his cap and bow back to them.

"We geese have been thinking," said Akka, "that if Thumbietot had been in the service of human beings and had done as much for them as he has for us, they would not let him go without rewarding him well."

"I haven't helped you—you have helped me," protested the boy.

"We also think," continued Akka, "that when a human being has accompanied us on a whole journey, he should not be allowed to leave us as poor as when he came."

"What I have learned this year with you is worth more than gold or lands," said the boy.

"Since these gold coins have been lying unclaimed in the cleft all these years, I think you ought to have them," declared the wild goose.

"Didn't you say something about needing the money your-selves?" reminded the boy.

"We do need it—to give you enough recompense to make your mother and father think you have been working as a goose-boy with worthy people."

The boy turned half-way round and cast a glance toward the sea, then faced about and looked straight into Akka's bright eyes.

"Mother Akka, are you turning me away from your service and paying me off before I have given notice?"

"As long as we wild geese remain in Sweden, I hope you will stay with us," said Akka. "I only wanted to show you where the treasure was while we could get to it without going too far off course."

"It still seems that you want me to leave before I want to go," argued Thumbietot. "After all the good times we've had together, I think you ought to let me go abroad with you."

Surprised by the news that he wanted to stay with them, Akka and the other wild geese stretched their long necks straight up and stood a moment with bills half open, drinking in air.

"That is something I haven't thought about," said Akka. "Before you decide to come with us, we had better hear what Gorgo has to say. When we left Lapland, the agreement between Gorgo and myself was that he should travel to your home down in Skåne to try to make better terms for you with the tomten."

"That's true," affirmed Gorgo, "but as I have already told you, luck was against me. I hunted up Holger Nilsson's farm and after circling up and down over the place a couple of hours, I caught sight of the tomten, sneaking between the sheds.

"I flew down on him and carried him off to a meadow where we could talk together without interruption. I told him I had been sent by Akka from Kebnekaise to ask if he wouldn't give Nils Holgersson easier terms.

"'I wish I could,' he answered, 'because I have heard that the boy has conducted himself well. It's just not in my power to give him better terms.'

"That made me angry, and I told him I'd bore out his eyes unless his gave in.

"'No matter what you do,' he said, 'it won't make things any better for Nils Holgersson. Tell him to return with his goose, because his father had to forfeit a bond for his brother, whom he trusted. Holger bought a horse with borrowed money, and the animal went lame the first time he drove it; since then it has been of no earthly use to him. Tell Nils, too, that his parents have had to sell two of the cows and that they must give up the farm unless they receive help from somewhere.'"

The boy frowned and clenched his fists so hard that the fingernails cut into his skin. "The tomten has made the conditions so hard that I can't go home and help my parents unless I betray a friend. I won't do that! My father and mother are honest people. I know they'd rather do without my help than have me return to them with a guilty conscience."

Chapter Twenty

The Journey to Vemminghög

Thursday, November third.
....

One day in the beginning of November, the wild geese flew over Halland Ridge and into Skåne. For several weeks they had been resting on the wide plains around Falköping. Since many other flocks of wild geese also stopped there, the adult geese had had a pleasant time visiting with old friends, and there had been all sorts of games and races among the goslings.

Nils Holgersson was still depressed after the day in Västergötland. "If only I were miles and miles away from Skåne, in some foreign land, I'd know for certain that I had nothing to hope for. Then I'd have nothing to lose, but as it is—"

Then one morning the geese started out and flew toward Halland. In the beginning, the boy took very little interest in that province. He didn't think there could be anything new to be seen there.

As the wild geese continued the journey farther south, along the narrow coastlands, the boy leaned over the goosey-gander's neck and saw the hills gradually disappear and the plain spread under him. The coast became less rugged, and the group of islands beyond thinned and finally vanished. The open sea went clear up to firm land. No forested land was to be seen, but the plain was supreme; it spread all the way to the horizon. A land that lay so exposed, with field upon field, reminded the boy of Skåne. Somehow he felt both happy and sad as he looked at it. "I can't be very far from home," he thought.

Many times during the trip the goslings had asked their parents, "What do foreign lands look like?"

"Wait now, wait! You'll soon see," the adult geese had assured them.

When the wild geese had passed Halland Ridge and gone into Skåne, Akka called out: "Look down! Look all around! This is what it's like in foreign lands."

They flew over Söder Ridge. The whole long range of hills was clad in beech woods, and beautiful, turreted castles peeped out here and there. Among the trees grazed roebuck, and on the forest meadow romped the hares. Hunters' horns sounded from the forests. The loud baying of dogs could be heard all the way up to the wild geese. Broad avenues wound through the trees, and on these ladies and gentlemen were riding in polished carriages or on fine horses. At the foot of the ridge lay Ring Lake, with the ancient Bosjö Cloister on a narrow peninsula.

"Are you sure it looks like this in foreign lands?" asked the goslings.

"It looks exactly like this wherever there are forest ridges," replied Akka, "but one doesn't see many of them. Wait another moment, and then you'll see how it looks in general."

Akka led the geese farther south to the great Skåne plain. There it spread, with lush grain fields; with acres and acres of sugar beets, where the beet pickers were at work; with low, white-washed farmhouses and outhouses; with little white churches; with ugly, gray sugar refineries and small villages near the railway stations. Little, beech-encircled meadow lakes—each of them adorned by its own stately manor—shimmered here and there.

"Look down! Look carefully!" called the leader goose. "This

is the way it is in foreign lands, from the Baltic coast all the way to the high Alps. That's as far as I've ever gone."

When the goslings had seen the plain, the leader goose flew down the Öresund coast. Swampy meadows sloped gradually toward the sea. In some places there were high, steep banks. In others there were fields of drifting sand, where the sand lay heaped in banks and hills. Fishing hamlets stood all along the coast—with long rows of low, uniform brick houses, with a lighthouse at the edge of the breakwater and brown fishing nets hanging in the drying yard.

"Look down! Look closely!" This is how it looks along the seacoasts in foreign lands."

After Akka had been flying for a long time, she alighted on a marsh in Vemminghög township. The boy could not help thinking that she had flown over Skåne to show him that his own country compared favorably with any other in the world.

From the moment that he had seen the first willow grove, his heart ached with homesickness.

Chapter Twenty-one

....

Home at Last

Tuesday, November eighth.

....

The sky was dull and hazy. The wild geese had been feeding on the meadow around Skerup church and were having their noonday rest, when Akka came up to the boy.

"It looks as if we'll have calm weather for awhile," she remarked, "so I think we'll cross the Baltic tomorrow."

"What?" The boy's throat contracted so he could hardly speak. All along he had hoped to be released from the enchantment while he was still in Skåne.

"We're near West Vemminghög," said Akka, "and I thought you might like to go home for awhile. It may be a long time before you have another chance to see your parents."

"I don't...know if I should," said the boy hesitatingly, but something in his voice let Akka know that he was glad that she had offered him this opportunity.

"If the goosey-gander remains with us, no harm can come to him," Akka went on. "See how your parents are getting along. You might be of help to them even if you aren't a normal boy."

"I think you're right. I should have thought of that long ago," said the boy.

Within a few minutes, he and the leader goose were on

their way to his home. When they got there, Akka alighted behind the stone hedge encircling the little farm.

Climbing to the top of the hedge so he could look around, the boy said, "I have the strangest feeling that it was only yesterday when I first saw you come flying through the air."

"Does your father have a gun?" asked Akka.

"Yes. It was his gun that kept me at home that Sunday morning when I should have been at church."

"Then I don't dare to wait for you," said Akka. "Meet us at Smygahök early tomorrow morning."

"Don't go yet, Mother Akka!" begged the boy. He couldn't tell why, but he sensed that something would happen, either to the wild goose or to himself, to prevent them from meeting again.

"I don't regret having gone with you last spring. I'd rather lose the chance of ever being human again than to have missed that trip."

Akka breathed quickly before replying. "If you have learned anything at all from us, Thumbietot, you no longer think that humans should have the whole world to themselves. Always remember that you have a large country and you can easily afford to leave a few bare rocks, a few shallow lakes and swamps, a few desolate cliffs and remote forests to us poor, dumb creatures— places where we can be allowed to live in peace. All my days I have been hounded and hunted. It would be a comfort to know that there is a refuge somewhere for one like me."

"Dear Mother Akka, you know I would help if I could, but I doubt that I'll ever have any influence among human beings."

"Well, we're standing here talking as if we were never to meet again," said Akka. "We shall see each other tomorrow, of course. I have to return to my flock now." She spread her wings and started to fly, but came back and stroked Thumbietot up and down with her bill before she flew away.

It was broad daylight, but no human being moved on the farm. Nils hurried to the cowshed, because he knew that he could get the best information from the cows.

The shed looked barren. In the spring there had been three

fine cows there, but now there was only one—Mayrose. It was quite apparent that she missed her friends. Her head drooped sadly, and she had hardly touched the feed in her crib.

"Good morning, Mayrose," said the boy, running into her stall. "How are Father and Mother? How are the cat and the chickens? Where are Star and Gold Lily?"

When Mayrose heard the boy's voice, she was startled, but she wasn't as quick-tempered as she used to be. She took time to get a good look at Nils Holgersson.

He was just as little now as when he went away, and he wore the same clothes. Yet he was completely different. The Nils Holgersson who went away in the spring had walked and talked slowly, and looked sleepy. The one who had come back was lithe and alert, talked fast and had eyes that sparkled and danced. He had a confident way about him that commanded respect, little as he was.

"Moo!" bellowed Mayrose. "I've heard you changed, but I couldn't believe it. Welcome home, Nils Holgersson. Welcome home. This is the first glad moment I have known for a long time."

"Thank you, Mayrose," said the boy, who was pleased to be so well received. "Tell me about Mother and Father."

"They have had nothing but misfortune since you left," she said. "The horse has been a costly responsibility all summer. He has stood in the stable the whole time and not earned his feed. Your father is too softhearted to shoot him, and he can't sell him. Because of the horse, both Star and Gold Lily had to be sold."

"Mother must have felt awful when Morton Goosey-Gander flew away."

"No, I can tell you she didn't worry much about Morton Goosey-Gander. She grieves most at the thought of her son having stolen the goosey-gander and run away."

"Is that what she thinks?"

"What else could she think?"

"Father and Mother think I have been roaming about the country...like a tramp?"

"They've mourned for you. They love you," Mayrose said.

The boy rushed from the cowshed and down to the stable.
The stable was small, but clean and tidy. Everything showed that
his father had tried to make the place comfortable for the new
horse. In the stall stood a strong, fine animal.

"Good morning," said the boy. "I've heard that there is a sick horse in here. It can't be you. You look strong and healthy."

The horse looked the boy up and down. "Are you the farmer's son?" he queried. "I have heard bad reports of him."

"I left a bad name behind me when I went away," admitted Nils. "My own mother thinks I'm a thief. It doesn't matter; I won't be here long. Before I leave, though, I'd like to know what's wrong with you. Are you sick?"

"I wish you'd stay," said the horse. "I have a feeling you and I could become good friends. Well, as for what's wrong with me, there's something in my foot—the point of a knife, or something sharp. It's gone so far in that the doctor can't find it, but it cuts me every time I try to walk.

"I'm sure your father could help me if he only knew what was wrong. I'd like to be of use to him. I'm ashamed to stand here and eat without doing any work."

"Maybe I can help," said Nils. "Would you mind if I did a little scratching on your hoof with my knife?"

The boy had just finished when he heard voices. His father and mother were coming down the lane. His mother's face had become wrinkled as though she had aged prematurely, and his father's hair had turned gray. Nils couldn't hear very clearly, but he thought his mother said something about getting a loan from her brother-in-law.

"I don't want to borrow any more money," his father said, as they were passing the stable. "There's nothing worse than being in debt. I'd rather sell the cabin."

"If it weren't for Nils, I wouldn't mind selling it," his mother demurred. "What will happen to him if he returns someday, wretched and poor, and we aren't here?"

"I don't know," the father said. "We'll have to ask the people who buy the place to receive him kindly and let him know that we would welcome him."

"If only I knew that he wasn't starving and freezing on the highways, I wouldn't ask for anything more," the mother added.

Then the two went into the house. He was deeply moved when he knew that they loved him so dearly. He wanted to rush into their arms and hug them. Oh, how he had missed them!

"But...maybe they would be even unhappier if they saw me the way I am now."

While he stood there, a cart drove up to the gate. The boy smothered a cry of surprise, for who should get out of the cart and go into the yard but Osa and her father!

They walked hand in hand toward the cabin. When they were about half-way there, Osa stopped and said, "Father, don't mention the wooden shoe or the geese, and please don't tell them about the little tomten who was so much like Nils Holgersson that if it weren't him, it must have had some connection with him."

"I won't, Osa," said Jon Esserson. "I'll only say that their son helped you on several occasions when you were trying to find me and that we have come to ask if we can't help them in return. Now that I'm a rich man, I have more than I need...thanks to the mine I discovered in Lapland."

They went into the cabin, and the boy would have liked to hear what they talked about, but he didn't dare go near the house. When they came out again, Nils' father and mother accompanied them as far as the gate.

They seemed happy. When the strangers had gone, Nils' parents lingered at the gate, gazing after them.

"They said so many wonderful things about our boy," said his mother.

"Maybe he got more praise than he deserved."

"Wasn't it enough that they came here to help us because our Nils had helped them? You should have accepted their offer."

"No, no. I won't accept money from anyone, either as a gift or a loan. I want to free myself from debt. Then we will work our way up again. We're not so very old, are we?"

Nils' father laughed heartily.

"I suppose you think it will be fun to sell this farm—after all the work and time we've invested in it," his wife protested.

"I'm not laughing about that," he replied. "The boy's having run away had been a burden to me. Now that I know he's alive and turned out to be a good boy, you'll find that Holger Nilsson has some grit left. What a relief!"

The mother went into the house alone, and Nils hid in a corner as his father entered the stable. Holger went over to the horse and examined its hoof, as usual, to see if he could find out what was wrong with it.

"Hm? What now?" he muttered in surprise when he saw some letters scratched on the hoof.

"Remove the sharp piece of iron," he read, glancing around to see if a stranger might be hiding somewhere. Then he ran his fingers along the underside of the hoof.

"Why, there *is* something sharp in here!" he exclaimed.

While his father was busy with the horse and the boy huddled in a corner, more visitors came to the farm.

The fact was that when Morton Goosey-Gander found himself so close to home, he simply couldn't resist the temptation to show his mate and goslings to his friends on the farm.

There wasn't a soul in the barnyard when the goosey-gander showed up. He alighted, confidently strutted all around the place, and showed Dunfin how luxuriously he had lived when he was a tame goose.

After they had toured most of the farm, the goosey-gander noticed that the door of the cowshed was open. "Let's look in here," he said.

From the doorway, the goosey-gander peered into the shed. "Come on, Dunfin. Don't be afraid. There's no danger."

Morton Goosey-Gander, Dunfin and all six goslings waddled into the goose pen to look at the luxury and comfort in which the big white gander had lived before he joined the wild geese.

"This is the way it used to be. Here was my place, and over there was the trough, which was always filled with oats and water.

"Look! There's fodder in it." He rushed to the trough.

"Let's go out again," Dunfin urged uneasily.

"Only two more grains," insisted the goosey-gander. The next second he let out a honk and ran for the door, but it was too late. The door slammed shut.

Nils' father had removed a sharp piece of iron from the horse's hoof and stood stroking the animal when the mother came running into the stable.

"Come and see what I've caught!"

"Look here, first. I've discovered what was wrong with the horse."

"Our luck has turned!" said Nils' mother. "The white goosey-gander that disappeared last spring must've gone off with the wild geese. He has returned with seven wild geese. They walked straight into the goose pen, and I've shut them in."

"So Nils didn't steal the gander!"

His wife nodded her head and smiled happily.

Then she remembered something. "We'll have to butcher the geese tonight. Morton Gooseday (November 10th, which in Sweden corresponds to the American Thanksgiving Day) is only two days away.

"We can't—not now that he's returned to us with such a large family."

"If times were better, we could let him live, but since we're going to move, we can't keep geese. Come and help me carry them into the kitchen."

They went out together, and in a few minutes the boy saw his father carrying Morton Goosey-Gander and Dunfin into the house.

"Thumbietot, help me! Thumbietot! Thumbietot!" honked the goosey-gander, as he always did when in peril, although he wasn't aware that the boy was near. "Thumbietot, help me!"

Nils heard him, but hesitated. What would his mother and father say if they saw him? But when the door shut, Nils couldn't hold back any longer. He dashed across the yard, jumped onto the boardwalk leading to the entrance and ran into the hallway, where he kicked off his wooden shoes in the old accustomed way. After all that he and the goosey-gander had gone through on ice-bound lakes and stormy seas and among wild beasts of prey—.

He knocked on the door.

"Yes?" asked his father, opening the door.

"Mother, don't touch the goosey-gander!" Nils shouted.

Instantly both the goosey-gander and Dunfin, who lay on a bench with their feet tied, cried with joy.

Someone else gave a cry—Nils' mother!

"Son!" she exclaimed. "Oh, my boy—Nils, you've grown so tall and handsome. The Lord be praised that I have you back." She laughed and cried at the same time. "Come in, my boy."

"Welcome!" added his father, and he couldn't utter another word.

Nils still stood in the doorway. He couldn't understand why they were glad to see him...such as he was. Then his mother came and put her arms around him and drew him into the room, and he knew that he was all right.

"Mother, Father!" he cried. "I'm big again! I am a human being."

THE TRAVELS OF

BOOK TWO

NILS HOLGERSSON

Chapter Twenty-two

The Parting With the Wild Geese

Wednesday, November ninth.
....

The boy got up before dawn and walked down to the sea-coast. He was standing alone on the strand east of Smyge fishing hamlet before sunrise. He had already been in the pen with Morton Goosey-Gander and tried to rouse him, but the big white gander had no desire to leave home. He poked his bill under his wing and went to sleep again.

To all appearances the weather would be almost as perfect as that spring day when the wild geese came to Skåne. There was hardly a ripple on the water, the air was still, and the boy thought of the good passage the geese would have. He himself was still in a kind of daze—sometimes thinking he was a tomten, sometimes a human being. When he saw a stone hedge along the road, he was afraid to go farther until he had made sure that no wild animal or vulture lurked behind it. Then he laughed to himself because he no longer needed to be afraid. When he reached the coast, he stood at the very edge of the strand so that the wild geese could see him.

It was a busy day for the birds of passage, and bird calls sounded on the air. The boy smiled, thinking that no one but himself understood what the birds were saying to one another. Soon wild geese came flying, one big flock following another.

"I hope Mother Akka and her flock won't leave without bidding me good-bye," Nils worried. He wanted to tell his friends how everything had turned out.

One flock flew faster and honked louder than the others, and he thought this must be the one he was looking for, but he

was not quite as certain about it as he would have been the day before. The flock slowed and circled up and down along the coast.

Now the boy knew it was the right one, but he could not understand why the geese did not come down to him. They could not avoid seeing him. He tried to think of a call that would bring them...but his tongue would not obey him. He could not make the right sound! He heard Akka's calls, but did not understand what she said.

"Have the wild geese changed their language?" he wondered.

He waved his cap to them and ran along the shore calling, "Here I am, where are you?" but the geese rose and flew farther out to sea.

At last Nils understood. They did not know that he had regained his human form, and they hadn't recognized him. He could not call them to him because human beings cannot speak the language of birds. He could not speak their language, nor could he understand it.

Although the boy was relieved to be released from the enchantment, he couldn't help being disappointed too; he missed his comrades. He sat down on the sand and dejectedly buried his face in his hands.

Then he heard the rustle of wings. Old Akka had found it hard to fly away from Thumbietot, and she'd turned back. Now that the boy sat quite still, she ventured to fly nearer to him.

Some of the enchantment must have returned, for suddenly she realized who he was and she lit close beside him.

Nils cried for joy and cradled her in his arms. The other wild geese crowded round him and stroked him with their bills. They cackled and honked and wished him all kinds of good luck, and he, too, talked to them and thanked them for the wonderful journey which he had been privileged to make in their company.

Then the spell lifted, and the wild geese withdrew from him, as if to say, "Alas! He is a human being. He cannot understand us, and we cannot understand him."

The boy went over to Akka, stroked her and patted her. He did the same to Yksi and Kaksi, Kolme and Neljä, Viisi and Kuusi—the birds who had been his companions from the very start. Then he turned away and walked up the strand. He knew that the sorrows of the birds do not last long, and he wanted to part with them while they were still sad at losing him.

As he crossed the shore meadows, he turned and watched the flocks of birds flying over the sea. All were shrieking their coaxing calls. Only one goose flock flew silently on as long as he could follow it with his eyes. The wedge was perfect, the speed good, and the wing strokes strong and certain.

The boy felt such a yearning for his departing friends that he almost wished he were Thumbietot again and could travel over land and sea with a flock of wild geese.

Map of Nils' Adventures

& Table of Pronunciation

Table of Pronunciation

The final *e* is sounded in Skåne, Sirle, Gripe, etc.

The å in Skåne and Småland is pronounced like *o* in ore.

j is like the English *y*. Nuolja, Oviksfjällen, Sjangeli, Jarro, etc., should sound as if they were spelled like this: Nuolya, Oviksfyellen, Syang(one syllable)elee, Yarro, etc.

g, when followed by *e, i, y, ä, ö*, is also like *y*. Example, Göta is pronounced Yöta.

When *g* is followed by *a, o, u*, or *å*, it is hard, as in go.

k in Norrköping, Linköping, Kivik (pronounced Cheeveek), etc., is like *ch* in cheer.

k is hard when it precedes *a, o, u*, or *å*. Example, Kaksi, Kolme, etc.

ä is pronounced like *ā* in fare. Example, Färs.

There is no sound in the English language which corresponds to the Swedish *ö*. It is like the French *eu* in jeu.

Gripe is pronounced Greep-e.

In Sirle, the first syllable has the same sound as *sir*, in sirup.

The names which Miss Lagerlöf has given to the animals are descriptive.*

Smirre Fox, is cunning fox.

Sirle Squirrel, is graceful, or nimble squirrel.

Gripe Otter, means grabbing or clutching otter.

Mons is a pet name applied to cats; like our tommy or pussy. Monsie house-cat is equivalent to Tommy house-cat.

Mårten gåskarl (Morton Goosie-gander) is a pet name for a tame gander, just as we use Dickie-bird for a pet bird.

Fru is the Swedish for Mrs. This title is usually applied to gentlewomen only. The author has used this meaning of "fru."

A Goa-Nisse is an elf-king, and corresponds to the English Puck or Robin Goodfellow.

VELMA SWANSTON HOWARD

---

*Editor's note: The names of *Yksi* from Vassijaure, *Kaksi* from Nuolja, *Kolme* from Sarjektjåkkå, *Neljä* from Svappavaara, *Viisi* from Oviksfjällen and *Kuusi* from Sjangeli—all high-mountain geese and members of Akka from Kebnekaise's flock—are Finnish words for one, two, three, four, five and six.

A Final Note

First published in 1907 as *Nils Holgerssons underbara resa genom Sverige*, *The Wonderful Adventures of Nils* by Selma Lagerlöf has been translated into more than thirty languages and read by children in more than thirty-five countries. One German edition alone has sold over seven million copies.

Book One in the two-volume set by Skandisk, Inc., published in 1991, begins the tale of a naughty boy who is changed into a tomten, caught on the back of a big, white goosey-gander and catapulted into the sky with a flock of wild geese, and enters a magical kingdom of well-educated, talking animals. With folklore, pure original fantasy and a profound understanding of the history and geography of Sweden, the first book spans the area from West Vemminghög Township, down in Southern Skåne, to the great Östergötland plain. This volume, Book Two, published in 1992, continues the saga of Nils Holgersson, develops the stories of other characters first found in Book One, and completes the amazing geography of Sweden.

Each book is enchanting in itself. Together, they are a remarkable saga of how a boy earns the trust and admiration of all who know him. It's a two-volume treasury of adventure and learning for the entire family.

NANCY JOHNSON